Mosaica Press, Inc.
© 2016 by Mosaica Press

Designed and typeset by Daniella Kirsch
All rights reserved
ISBN-10: 1-937887-73-1
ISBN-13: 978-1-937887-73-5

No part of this publication may be translated, reproduced, stored in a retrieval system or transmitted in any form or by any means, electronic, mechanical, photocopying, recording, or otherwise, without prior permission in writing from both the copyright holder and the publisher.

Published and distributed by:
Mosaica Press, Inc.
www.mosaicapress.com
info@mosaicapress.com

ACKNOWLEDGMENTS

This story was born in my classroom in Providence, Rhode Island. After two years, it is finally complete!

I thank my students Ze'ev, Gavriel, Meir Mordechai, and Azriel, for encouraging me to write chapter after chapter every week!

I thank Rabbi Yaakov Zimmerman, my friend and advisor, for the development of many aspects of this book.

I am full of gratitude to my dear friend Rabbi Shmuel Taitelbaum, whose constant expressions of praise motivate me to be creative.

Words of thanks do not suffice for my children, who laugh at my jokes and encourage my storytelling. I love you so much and I am so proud of you!

My supportive siblings and their families deserve to be mentioned too. Thanks, Chaim, for keeping the family ties strong; Mindy Shapiro, for providing storytelling opportunities; Esther-Miriam Benyowitz, for inspiring me with your *bitachon*; Dovid, for inspiring my *chavivus* for Eretz Yisrael; and Ovadiah, for tech support and financial guidance. Thanks, Devorah, for all you do for our family.

I owe so much to my in-laws, Rabbi and Mrs. Avrohom and Lynn Jakubowicz. Thank you for bringing me to Providence and helping me to become a *rebbi*!

Yasher koach to my siblings-in-law for all the inspiration you constantly provide my family.

In my last conversation before my mother, Fagie Yudkowsky *a"h* was *nifteres*, I discussed various elements of the plot. I am sad that she could not read the completed story, but I am comforted knowing that she was so proud of my various projects. *Yb"l*, my father, Rabbi Reuven Yudkowsky, stands behind me in all of my ideas and plans, and helped make this book a reality. Thank you, Daddy, I love you.

A special word of *hakaras ha-tov* is due to Rabbi Shlomo and Mrs. Tamar Rechnitz and Rabbi Itche Rosenbaum. Their generous investment in this book and belief in my mission as a *rebbi* is motivating.

This book is dedicated to my wife, Shiffy. She is a powerhouse; a bundle of energy and *chesed*. Her care and devotion to her students and the Providence community is inspiring. Her dedication to and focus on being the best mother is uplifting. Her faith in me and pride in my position as *rebbi* reflect her most outstanding feature: being the greatest wife!

I am indebted to Mrs. Bracha Steinberg, Mrs. Sherie Gross, Doron Kornbluth, and the entire staff of Mosaica Press for helping the story become a book. Wow! I can't believe it really happened!

I end by expressing gratitude to the Ribbono shel Olam for all that He has bestowed upon me and for granting me the ability to help change the world with *When the Ice Melts*.

Dedicated to my wife,

Shiffy

PROLOGUE

Sitting on the roof next to the chimney, with blood dripping from the gash in his forehead, eight-year-old Josh watched with fascinating horror. A black wall of water twenty feet tall was racing across the beach that separated his home from the waters of the Atlantic Ocean. From the relative safety of his perch up so high, Josh saw the water swallow the wooden boat docks, and next, the beach shower houses, and then wildly make its way toward his house.

It was then that Josh heard the *womp-womp* sound of helicopter rotors. Looking up, Josh saw a camouflage-clad National Guardsman being lowered by the chopper's[1] winch. Frightened, Josh began to inch his way toward the window of his second-floor bedroom.

The Guardsman gesticulated wildly to Josh. Josh ignored him and continued on so that he could reenter his flooding home. Concentrating on each step so as not to slip, Josh moved an inch at a time, slowly, toward the window.

Suddenly, his focus was jarred by a tugging on his arm. Josh looked at his wrist and saw the black-gloved hand of the Guardsman clasped like a vise around it.

---
[1] Slang for "helicopter."

The soldier shouted above the loud noise of the crashing waves. "My name is Sergeant Collins. I am here to rescue you. It isn't safe for you to go back into your home now. Let me put this safety harness on you and we'll go for a ride in my helicopter!"

Without giving Josh a chance to refuse, Sergeant Collins fastened the harness on him. He then motioned to the pilot, and the winch began to hoist the rescuer together with the rescued.

As he was rising into the sky, Josh was unable to take his eyes off his home. He watched as a second wave of water rushed toward it. Suddenly, Josh let out a cry of anguish! The force of the wave swept the house off of its foundation, and water completely covered it. Then the tremendous weight of the water caused his magnificent home to explode into a million pieces, as if it had been made of matchsticks!

Sergeant Collins loaded Josh onto the helicopter and gently laid him down on a cot that was attached to the wall. Josh had felt safe in the Guardsman's arms. Slowly, a heavy darkness began to envelope him. He struggled to stay alert and focused, but the weight of his eyelids was just too much and his eyes closed.

The sergeant saw the boy's body go limp on the bed. Shouting above the noise in the cabin, Collins called for the flight surgeon, Dr. MacMallean. "Hey, Doc! I think the boy is losing consciousness!"

The doctor rushed over. Abruptly, from the edge of consciousness, Josh felt his pupils blinded by sudden light. Dr. MacMallean stood above Josh and shined his penlight into the patient's eyes.

"So what do you think?" Collins asked, fearing the worst.

The flight surgeon answered in a loud, but reassuring, voice, "See how his pupils are dilated? His heart rate is also way down. His skin is cold and clammy. Clearly the boy is going into shock!"

With his voice betraying his worry, Collins asked, "Will he be all right?"

"Sure! As soon as he gets an infusion of some saline solution to raise his blood pressure, he should stabilize. I'm also dressing the cut on his head. But he needs stitches and there could be other issues. We really need to get him to a hospital stat.[2] What's our ETA?[3]"

Collins punched the button on his helmet that patched him through[4] to the pilots. "ETA?" he asked.

"Ten minutes or so," replied the pilot.

"Okay. Let's try to make it in five!" Collins answered.

As they flew toward the hospital, Collins and the doctor gazed out of the windows. The sight was horrible. Beneath them, the city was devastated. Block after block was flooded. Hundreds of homes lay in ruins. The chopper was racing past families perched on their rooftops awaiting rescue. As they flew by, each group would look up as if in supplication, begging for the medivac helicopter to rescue them. The silent plea tore at the heartstrings of the doctor.

"Let's ask the pilot to pick up others," MacMallean ventured. "There's more room in here!"

Sergeant Collins shook his head. "No can do. We've reached our weight limit. In this weather, any more weight would hamper our ability to fly safely. Even rescuing the boy was risky. But, like you, I couldn't pass him by. Also, about twenty different government organizations are here with their aircrafts and amphibious vehicles to join in the rescue. Help will arrive for them soon."

The doctor and the soldier continued to stare outside. Casual conversation was nearly impossible even with their headsets, but the tears that flowed steadily down their cheeks expressed their mutual thoughts: *How did this happen? What caused this terrible tragedy? How could it be that in the middle of the twenty-first century, with all our science and technology, we can't prevent such catastrophes?*

---

2   Hospital term for "immediately."
3   Estimated time of arrival.
4   Slang for "connected via a phone or walkie-talkie."

Finally the aircraft approached JFK Memorial Hospital. The pilot slowed his flight to forty knots about a quarter of a mile from the landing zone. Carefully lowering the collective,[5] the pilot slowed his aircraft until he gently settled his three-ton rescue vehicle exactly in the center of the *X* on the roof of the hospital's pediatric wing.

The rotors slowed as the pilot powered down the engine. Suddenly, as if shot from a cannon, doctors and nurses came crashing through the LZ's[6] double doors. They moved in practiced choreography, transferring the small boy from his cot in the chopper into the triage[7] area for a medical assessment.

Sergeant Collins stayed with Josh the entire time. While he was waiting, Collins searched the boy's pockets and found a soggy, but legible, paper with emergency contact information for the boy.

The sergeant placed a call to the cell phone number listed and reached Josh's hysterical parents. They had gone away just for the day, leaving Josh with one of the neighbors. "When the storm intensified," Josh's mother explained, "our neighbors gathered their family members to evacuate the area and they couldn't find Josh! They tried to look for him, but the authorities were pressuring everyone to leave, and they eventually left without him! Of course they called us right away and we wanted to go home to search the area for our son."

Josh's parents explained that they could not return because all the roads were blocked, and no pleading, begging, or cajoling could get them past the police barricades.

"It was only a little while ago that one of the neighbor's children remembered that Josh had said he was going home to get something!" Josh's mother ended her detailed, guilt-ridden speech with a sharp intake of breath.

---

5 This controls the up-and-down movements of the helicopter.
6 Landing zone.
7 Where a patient's medical priority is determined.

"Very understandable." Sergeant Collins hoped that this was the appropriate response to the details shared with him. He then assured Josh's parents that the boy was safe and in good hands, and he received their verbal permission to move forward with Josh's medical treatment.

After a thorough examination, six stitches, and an MRI,[8] Josh was wheeled into a quieter part of the ER.[9] By now, the darkness that had descended upon him to help hide his misfortune had lifted. Josh was again fully conscious. Seeing panic begin to register in Josh's face, Sergeant Collins reached out and grabbed hold of his hand. Collins squeezed gently and whispered, "Remember me? We were together in the helicopter. I know all of this is scary. But don't worry. My job is to protect people in scary situations. I will be by your side. I spoke to your parents and they will be here soon. Okay? Squeeze back if you understand me."

Josh tightly squeezed the sergeant's hand. In a fragile and trembling voice, Josh uttered quietly, "Thank you so much."

Sergeant Collins was deeply touched by the manners of a boy who was living through such a traumatic experience.

---

8 Magnetic resonance imaging is a diagnostic tool that uses magnetic fields and pulses of radio wave energy to produce detailed pictures of structures in the body.
9 Emergency room.

CHAPTER ONE

To an outside observer looking at 3387 Northern Parkway, the red brick building sitting on the corner of the busy intersection of Northern Parkway and Reisterstown Road was just another casualty of the failing economy in Baltimore's northeast section. Etched into the stain-streaked limestone lintel above the entrance, a hint to a more glorious past, was the name: Le Chateau. The lower two floors had boards covering their windows. The walls of the remaining three floors were tagged with the artwork of a graffiti artist. Broken glass liquor bottles, marking the frequent visits by vagrants, littered the yard. The big padlock on the front door did little to keep unwanted creatures from entering through the holes in the brickwork. Everything about the building cried out "abandoned."

Across the street, Pinny Gelbtuch was in his usual spot selling candy bars. He wanted to raise money for a trip with his eighth-grade class to Philadelphia. Pinny took his job quite seriously. He had built himself a collapsible table out of wood. Every day, with his wares secured in his backpack, he would place the folding table under his arm and shlep four blocks from his home to "his" corner. He would set up the table and neatly line up the candy bars like soldiers on review. Pinny even printed small business cards with his name and home phone number. The cards invited customers to preorder if they had any special requests.

Usually, the busy lawyers, politicians, and office workers, racing to get from somewhere to nowhere, would speed past his booth, plop a dollar or two on the table, grab a bar, and keep moving, calling behind them that Pinny could keep the change. There were a couple of customers who liked to schmooze. One talker was a window washer. His name was Fred, and he was known to be "the best washer in the business." Fred was also known for his really punny sense of humor. Lately, Pinny had groaned a lot in mock anguish at Fred's jokes. Like the one about the fellow who couldn't use his coffee mug after he'd told it a joke. The mug had cracked up!

Another friendly customer was Mr. Silver, an elderly lawyer. Mr. Silver davened in the same shul as Pinny and his father, and was liked by everyone there. Over the half century that he had practiced law, Mr. Silver had cultivated strong friendships with very powerful people. His word was golden, and his advice was sought on nearly every community matter. Mr. Silver admired Pinny's entrepreneurship, and he made it a point to stop by for a chat and some chocolate almost every day. In the few hours a day that Pinny stood at the corner, he would sell thirty or more bars.

Today, however, business was really slow. It was cold. There was a dampness lingering in the air from the previous night's rain. People seemed to be hurrying down the block even faster than usual. Nobody was willing to stop for, what they deemed on days like today, an annoying entrepreneur. In addition, the sun was beginning its short journey below the horizon; darkness was slowly filtering into the day's end. Pinny debated closing his shop for the day and heading home.

I sold ten bars out of my box, Pinny said to himself. *Even at this rate per day, I'll be able to raise what I need for the trip. Especially because we will be having the raffle fundraiser in a month or so. I might as well go home.*

Pinny carefully collected the merchandise from the table and placed it in his backpack. He then folded the table and placed it firmly under his arm. It was as he was turning to head down the block that Pinny's eyes caught the movement by Le Chateau.

Climbing the ivy-covered fire escape of the old ruin was a man. Had the man looked like a beggar, Pinny would not have displayed any interest in this person. However, even at a distance, Pinny could see that he was well-dressed and clean-shaven.

Unable to contain his curiosity, Pinny hurried to stow his table and candy behind an old couch in a nearby alleyway. Then he deftly jumped the fence that surrounded the building and began to creep up the fire escape, well behind Mystery Man, who did not turn around or indicate in any way that he had heard anyone else. Upon reaching the fourth-floor landing, the man opened the fire door and entered the building. A minute later, Pinny followed.

What he saw inside stunned him.

Wow! Pinny thought, *this is the coolest room ever!*

The huge room, which looked like a factory loft, was filled with all types of paraphernalia. From the ceiling hung at least half a dozen different 3-D models of the planetary system, scaled by feet and not inches. Also hanging from the ceiling was a series of nozzles attached to long garden hose-like tubes which snaked their way across the ceiling toward the plumbing on the far wall. On that same wall, together with the plumbing, were affixed dials, knobs, and gauges. It was as if someone had taken a wall panel from a submarine control room and transplanted it here. To his right, Pinny saw a bank of computers and printers, some of which were humming with activity and controlled by some invisible force. Toward his left, Pinny saw old crates and boxes apparently abandoned by an earlier tenant. All the walls were painted industrial gray, and in the middle of the floor sat a large antique desk upon which rested the largest globe that Pinny had ever seen. Standing by the office chair next to the desk was Pinny's man of interest.

The mystery man was rifling through some papers with his back to the door. As quietly as possible, Pinny tiptoed over to one of the large crates that was resting in the shadows not far from where he had entered. He thought he would sit there—a good distance from the man—and hopefully remain undetected while he continued to observe. He wanted to figure out whether the man was up to no-good.

Just as he was settling in for a long watch, Pinny's foot accidentally sent a pebble clattering away, the sound of its bouncing along the concrete floor carrying throughout the room. Pinny froze. He was too frightened to move. Many jumbled thoughts coursed through his thirteen-year-old mind: *Was that loud enough for the man to notice? Is he going to look in my direction? Will I be caught? Why did I let my curiosity lead me here?*

"Come on out, Pinny," the man called. "Don't be frightened. I won't harm you."

Pinny didn't move. He already regretted his hasty decision to enter this building. He knew that if his mother ever found out that he had acted so impulsively, he would find himself grounded for at least a year! To come out and show himself to the stranger would violate one of his mother's cardinal rules: Don't talk to strangers unless there are other adults nearby. It would likely earn him a grounding until his eighteenth birthday! Pinny looked the whole room over, wondering if he should simply run out the way he had come in.

Pinny's thoughts were interrupted. "Really, I won't hurt you. I'll even let you leave without talking to me, if you want. I'm going around now to the other side of my desk. I'll keep my hands on my desk and, as you can see, I'm not holding a weapon of any sort. You may leave my office and I won't stop you. However, on your way out, I'd like to speak to you for a minute, if you're not too afraid."

Pinny stood up and, with slow and uncertain steps, made his way toward the faded, unlit exit sign above the metal fire door. He purposely did not turn his head toward the desk. He was worried about what would happen if he made eye contact with the mystery man.

As his hand was ready to depress the push bar fastened across the middle of the door, Pinny could no longer contain his curiosity. He turned around and asked, "How do you know my name?"

The mystery man began to chuckle. "Don't you recognize me? I'm one of your best customers!"

Seeing the confusion on Pinny's face, the man continued, "Candy. Isn't that your business? I buy at least two chocolate bars a day from you! I even have one of your business cards right here!" Smiling, the man picked up Pinny's card from the desk and gave it a small wave.

Pinny felt his face redden. He was always so focused on making enough money for his class trip that he rarely paid attention to the individuals buying the candy. It wouldn't matter to him if the president of the United States came up to his table; as long as he was making a sale, Pinny was not even thinking about who his customers were.

"I'm sorry I don't recognize you," Pinny said. "You see, I have so many customers that I have trouble remembering them all. Well, I appreciate your business, but I gotta go now." With a sudden burst of energy, Pinny threw the door open and fled down the fire escape.

Josh Green watched the door slam shut. He walked around the desk and sat down before a computer. His cheery face that had been displayed to Pinny was altered into one of intense focus. He looked at the screen and began to compose an e-mail.

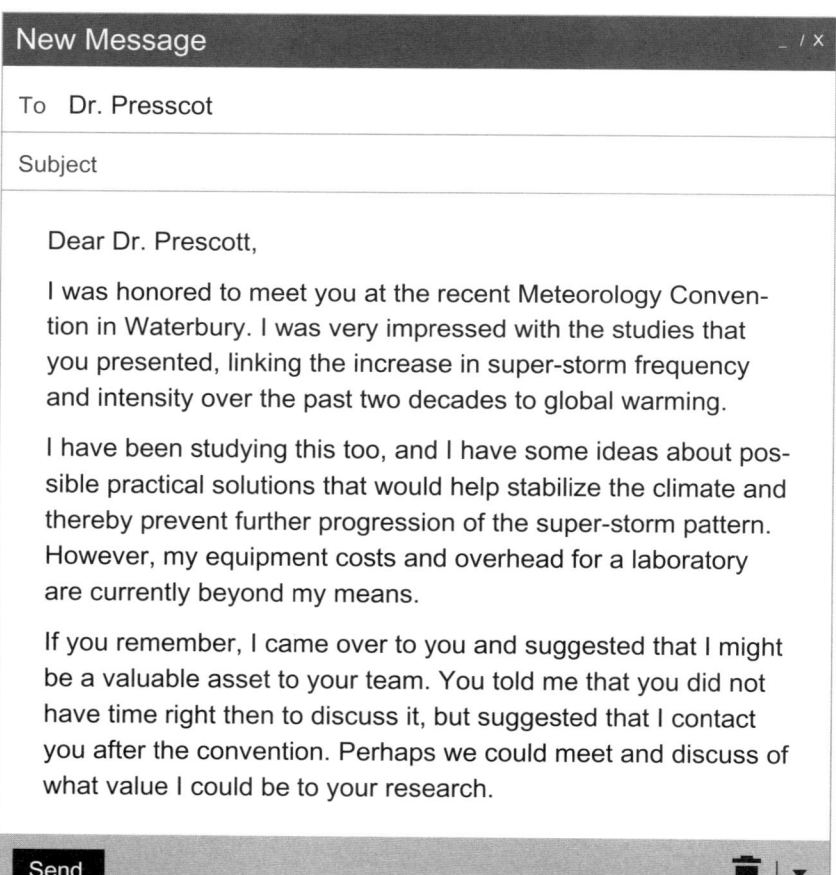

Josh signed his name and pressed the Send button. As he powered down his equipment and made his way out the door, he sighed. His life was way too boring. His focus on science had turned him into a geek who engaged in very little social interaction. As he closed and locked his fire door, Josh reflected on the young man who had visited a few moments ago. *I think the shock of that kid coming up to my office was the most exciting thing that's happened to me in months! Boy, I really need to get a life!*

CHAPTER TWO

He found himself in the semidarkness of dusk and began searching for the alleyway in which he had stowed his belongings. There were three of them close to the fire escape, and in his haste to follow the mysterious fellow, Pinny had not checked the street sign before hiding his stuff. Finally, after fifteen minutes of searching, Pinny had his wares. By now it was completely dark and he was late. He knew exactly what to expect when he arrived at home.

Pinny walked the four blocks back to his house at a brisk pace. The eight-minute walk only took five. Pinny arrived at his semidetached, red brick home, punched in the combination on the front door lock, and quietly pushed the door open. He figured there was a chance that he might be able to sneak into the house without his mother realizing that he was so late.

I know that sneaking inside isn't honest, Pinny thought, *but in this situation, maybe it falls into the category of sakanas nefashos!*

Pinny entered the small orange and yellow foyer, stepped over his siblings' coats that were strewn across the floor, and began to cross the "dangerous" area of "open terrain"—the ten feet before the stairs leading to his bedroom. Step-by-step, Pinny tiptoed unobserved.

He reached the steps and placed his right foot on the bottom one to begin his ascent. Pinny was rejoicing in his mind, *I made it, baruch Hashem. Whew. That was close!*

Suddenly, Pinny's mother spotted him with her maternal radar. "Pinny, do you know what time it is?" she cried out. She was in a state of controlled panic.

"Pinny," his mother continued, "it's after six o'clock. Where were you? Do you know how worried I've been?"

"But Ma," Pinny tried to squeeze in a response between his mother's hysterics, "I was–"

"And it's dark outside. Just last week the Greenbaums had a window broken by some hoodlum."

"I know, Ma, but the police–"

"And don't you remember the alert that was sent out on the JBAL[10] e-mail about the boys who were bothered in the Har Sinai parking lot?"

Chana Gelbtuch's words of rebuke went on and on. Pinny gave up. He did not even try to explain. This was *so* typical. Pinny would do something

---

10 Name of the e-mail group for Jews in Baltimore for sharing information concerning the community.

wrong and his mother would lecture him and ask questions without waiting for any answers. Usually in these situations, if his mother really wanted him to answer, she would pause for a few moments.

Pinny sighed. He understood his mother's concern. Pinny and his family lived in a run-down neighborhood. The streets were populated with a combination of Jews and other minorities. Though they were different from each other in many ways, the citizens of this community shared poverty as a common denominator.

There. I admitted it, Pinny thought. *My family is poor. That's why we live in a place that worries my mother so much. So many of my issues come from our financial challenges. Take the baseball glove that I have; it's so worn-out that...*

"Are you listening, Pinny? Answer me, please!"

His mother's question startled Pinny, stopping him from wallowing in a sea of self-pity. Guessing that his mother was finally asking him for the story behind his late arrival, Pinny explained.

"Well, Ma, I told you that I was selling candy bars and...." Pinny tried to figure out what to say next. How was he going to explain even the innocent parts of the story, like misplacing his table and backpack, without revealing how he had foolishly followed a stranger into a building? Was this a case, maybe, where it would be permissible to lie for the sake of *shalom*, to prevent a big fight? Should he call a Rav and ask a *shailah*, a halachic question?

I wonder what Mommy would say if I told her that I can only answer after I call the Rav to find out if it's okay for me to lie. Pinny almost laughed out loud at this thought. He didn't realize that his face was betraying what he was thinking.

"Pinny, if you think this is funny, then there are going to be some serious consequences! When Tatty comes home from work, we will sit down and discuss responsibility. I can't believe it. I was so sure that once you reached bar-mitzvah age, you would show more *seichel* and maturity." Pinny's mother walked away shaking her head.

Pinny felt bad. Finally, he had a kind of a good explanation and he couldn't share it! Pinny had been irresponsible in the past. He had trouble getting to where he needed to be, when he needed to be. He often got in trouble in school for his impulsive actions that upset his teacher or the *menahel*. Pinny had explained to the *menahel*, Rabbi Finegold, that Hashem had given his brain a slower processing speed than that of his body. That's why it often happened that before he thought of the consequence, he had already done the deed.

That explanation came to Pinny while sitting in the *menahel*'s office. Why was he there? He had pulled in a length of one of the school's watering hoses (the kind with little holes punched in it so the water would slowly drip from it into the flowerbed) from the side of the building and up through the top of one of his classroom's windows. He had also set the timer to turn the water on at the time that his class would be up to Shemoneh Esrei, so that his class would remember to daven for rain (get it?). When the artificial rain arrived, the result didn't just remind his classmates of raindrops. It reminded his classmates of just how much one student could get in trouble for such a prank.

Well, the *menahel* did not accept this explanation for his actions. Neither did his parents when they picked him up for his two-day suspension. But that was old news. Water under the bridge.

Since becoming bar mitzvah in the summer, Pinny was trying to do things right. He was *trying* to be on time. He was *trying* to be the responsible, mature, and perfect young man that his parents expected him to be. But nobody is perfect, and so, at times, Pinny fell back on his old ways.

Oh well, Pinny thought. *I hope Tatty will be busy tonight with some customers and then this whole thing will blow over.*

Pinny went up to his room to do some homework before supper.

Pinny shared his room with his four younger brothers. The room was relatively small, with a closet covering the entire wall opposite

Chapter Two 25

the door. Walking into the room, one was flanked on the immediate right and left by two bunk beds standing tall and proud. They bore the marks of honorable service, much like ships that sail through typhoons (hence the water stains), army tanks that blast their way to victory (hence the gouges in the wood), and rocket ships that fly to the edges of the solar system (hence the abundance of old bubble gum and candy wrappers). A large window, covering half the distance from the ceiling to the floor, decorated the middle of the right side wall. The potential room-enhancing benefit of this big window was diminished by a loft bed attached to this wall on either side of the window. The bed was further supported by two posts about six feet tall, with small horizontal boards nailed across one of the posts to serve as a ladder for the occupant to climb into bed.

This was Pinny's domain. Directly under the loft bed was a space for doing homework. With the help of Ikea, Pinny's parents had managed to squeeze in a desk and a bookcase, together with a pair of yellowish beanbags, despite it being a very tight and cramped space. Bearing the words "Homework Nook," a crude sign taped above the desk proclaimed the name of this well-used work space.

Most of the floor space was cluttered with toys. However, there was a patch of worn-out, brown carpet in the middle of the room that managed to serve as the boys' play area.

Pinny headed toward the Homework Nook. He passed his brothers, who were building some sort of Lego city.

"Wanna play?" three-year-old Yechiel asked sweetly.

"Maybe later," Pinny answered. "I've got homework to do."

Pinny sat down, took his binder from his backpack, and opened it to his *Chumash* questions. He read the first question. "List the twenty-four gifts that the Kohen receives." The question was followed by twenty-four lines. Pinny's hand was tired just from thinking about writing the answer. Instead, Pinny just sat there and started to doodle.

"What are you drawing?" His eight-year-old brother's question snapped Pinny out of his trance. He looked at the page, and much to his surprise, saw that he had drawn an imperfect picture of the funny instrument he had seen on a shelf in the mystery man's office.

"Nothing," Pinny answered.

Pinny continued to sit at the desk, deep in thought. It had been really foolish and even dangerous to enter that building. Looking back, Pinny was horrified by his decision to follow a perfect stranger into such a secluded, unsafe place. Still, he wasn't planning on saying anything about it to his mother. To be upset with himself was one thing. To make his mother upset with him was another.

Minutes later, the boys heard their mother's call to supper. They all hurried downstairs to the kitchen, eager to eat the night's special: macaroni and cheese. As Pinny descended the stairs, he kept a sharp lookout for his father. Not seeing him, Pinny headed for the kitchen. He picked up a plate from the table and began to scoop out a teenager-size portion of the macaroni. His mother was standing by the sink scrubbing the noodle pot clean.

"Is Tatty home yet?" he asked her.

"No. Actually, Tatty called to say that there was a lot of traffic on the Jones Falls Expressway, so he won't be home for at least another half hour."

Pinny breathed a sigh of relief. Tonight he had *mishmar*, so he would be gone by the time his father got home. His father went to a Daf Yomi *shiur* while he was at *mishmar* and only returned home after Pinny was in bed. He was safe from more lecturing at least for tonight.

CHAPTER THREE

The warm rays of the morning sun radiated through the window, casting their natural light on Pinny's face and penetrating the eyelids that were preserving his dreamless slumber. Pinny's hands instinctively reached for his black-and-gray quilt and pulled it over his head.

Pinny's attempt to gain a few extra minutes of sleep was foiled by his mother's piercing voice from downstairs. "Pinny, it's late! You need to get up now, *zeeskeit*. You only have twenty-five minutes until the carpool picks you up for Shacharis."

Pinny grunted an acknowledgment to his mother's call and rolled over, wrapping his blanket tightly against his body. He was sure that he could snooze for another ten minutes and still make his ride. His second attempt at getting some extra sleep was interrupted by little feet stepping on his stomach.

"Ouch!" Pinny shouted. He took the blanket off his head to see Moishe, his six-year-old brother, standing on his stomach. "What are you doing? You're hurting me!" Pinny complained as he sat up in bed.

"Mommy told me to see if you're up. So I was going to check your eyeballs. But now that you sat up, I know that you're awake!" Moishe said.

Grumbling and murmuring Modeh Ani, Pinny climbed down the ladder at the end of his bed. Before stepping off the last rung, Pinny reached out with his right foot and inserted it into its slipper. Pinny then looked for the left one. It was not at the foot of the ladder, waiting like the obedient servant it usually was. Careful not to put his bare foot on the floor, Pinny hopped around the room looking for the elusive slipper. It was nowhere to be found. Pinny gave up, slipped his arms into the sleeves of his bathrobe, and walked with one foot shoeless on the cold wood floor into the bathroom in order to wash his hands.

As he limped along, Pinny remembered that once, when his friend Alex had slept at his house, Alex had questioned Pinny about his *negel vasser* habits. "Didn't we learn that you should keep your *negel vasser* cup and bowl by your bed so you don't need to walk far to wash when you wake up in the morning?" he had asked. "Why don't you keep some on the shelf by the head of your bed?"

Later, Pinny asked his *rebbi* about this. His *rebbi* had explained that in a house with little kids who might end up spilling the water from *negel vasser*, the halachah is lenient and allows a person to wash in a sink.

Chapter Three   29

Pinny shook the cobwebs of sleep from his head, grabbed the knob to the bathroom door, and tried to twist it. It was locked. Pinny knocked heavily on the door. "Who's in there? Come on. I'm in a rush!" he called in a gruff, gravelly voice.

When nobody answered the knock, Pinny tried again, banging on the door with his closed fist. This time the door flew open. Pinny's fourteen-year-old sister, Chedva, came out with her hair wrapped in a towel. "Pinny," she said sternly, "you know that your time for the bathroom in the morning is 6:20. Well, I waited and waited, and at 6:35 I just went in. If you're late, you can't make it my problem."

Pinny didn't answer her. He just nodded his head and brushed his way past Chedva into the bathroom.

The rest of the morning routine was fraught with difficulties. Pinny tripped on the way down the stairs, spilled the milk all over his mother's recently mopped floor while retrieving his lunch from the refrigerator, and forgot his coat at home as he shot out of the house to avoid missing the carpool. When his friend's lunch box bumped Pinny's head while he was climbing to the back seat of the van, Pinny decided that as soon as he arrived at school, he would go to the office to call his mother to come and take him home. He figured that if all of these disasters could happen in the first half hour of the day, he'd be safer in bed! But Pinny knew from experience that although she really loved him, she would not come for him. Instead, he would hear a masterfully crafted talk full of words of encouragement and enthusiasm, explaining how facing challenges on tough days builds character and would make Pinny a better person.

Not worth it, thought Pinny. *I just need to remember to daven extra hard that the rest of the day will be better.*

After first period ended, Pinny regretted his decision to stick it out.

Pinny went to a private school that leased a building from the city. The only reason that the building had not yet been demolished was the steady revenue from the lease that filled the coffers of the city, and maybe even the pockets of a couple of politicians. The building showed its age in many ways. Take the library, for instance. The books inside it deserved the attention of a rare books collector, not middle-school boys. More significant was the section roped off to protect visitors to this repository of knowledge from the possible collapse of the ceiling.

The hallways also showcased the age of this relic. In the olden days, the fire code only required that the hallways be five or six feet wide. Now, with the modern bulky backpacks that were often unable to fit into the lockers lying around the hall, and the 250 students moving through a building designed for just 100 or so, the corridor was quite crowded.

Pinny was walking in one of these narrow passageways, intending to quench his thirst. He was carrying his report on the Chofetz Chaim that he had shown his *rebbi*. Pinny was really proud of the time he had invested in the report and felt confident that he would get a good grade. His *rebbi* agreed that it was well written and deserved the highest mark. As he strolled down the hall, Pinny was—like most of the boys in his school often did—looking at the various projects the teachers displayed on the walls outside of their classrooms. Pinny was not watching where he was going. Consequently, Pinny bumped into his worst friend. Literally. Eli Truxenberg was a person one could not afford not to befriend. He was big, strong, and mean. In short, Eli was a bully. Bumping into anybody is embarrassing. Bumping into Eli was dangerous.

"Excuse me!" bellowed Eli. "Look who can't see in front of his nose! Pinny Winny! So, apologize! Ask me *mechilah*! Go down on one knee. Look up at me and say, 'My friend and favorite classmate, *Eli*, I am so sorry for being a little inconsiderate boy. Please can you forgive me?'"

Pinny didn't want to follow Eli's command. His pride was at stake. Slowly, he looked around to see if there was any rescue in sight. Maybe a *rebbi* or teacher was nearby. Or, maybe another boy would help him out. But as Pinny looked around, he found no adult in the area. None of the boys who stopped to watch would meet his eye, indicating that even his real friends in the hall were not going to help him. Pinny had no choice. He did what Eli demanded. Pinny went down on one knee and said, "*My friend and favorite classmate, Eli*, I am so sorry for being a little inconsiderate boy. Please can you forgive me?"

Eli burst out laughing and then, with a cold gleam in his eye and a cruel smile on his lips he replied, "No! I don't forgive you. Ask me a different time when there are more people around. Like at lunch. Today!"

With that, Eli turned and nonchalantly walked away. Pinny quickly hid his face. He did not want anyone to see the tears that were coursing down his cheeks. All Pinny could think about was how he was going to avoid the lunchroom at noon.

CHAPTER FOUR

As Pinny walked the four blocks to set up his chocolate stand that afternoon, he was still teary-eyed. Pinny's pain and embarrassment that day in school had not ended with the awful scene at lunch that Pinny had not been able to avoid. The school day had ended with Pinny seeing his low grade—a 36—on his math test, and subsequently, a talk from the principal about trying harder. At least now he would be able to relax.

Pinny set up shop at the corner next to the low stone wall, following his usual procedure. The routine of lining up the candy bars had a calming effect on him. Pinny had just placed the last of the forty candy bars—a Snickers bar— in its spot when the first customer arrived. Pinny was kept busy for quite a few minutes, stuffing bills into his pocket, giving change, expressing thanks to the buyers, and filling the bald spots in his candy presentation.

With the initial rush over, Pinny pulled out the wad of cash from his pocket and eagerly counted his money. He had done well. He had earned more in the past half hour than the average worker at Walmart earned in a day! Pleased with his success and waiting for the next customer, Pinny sat down on the stone wall and dreamed about being rich.

He imagined living in a home where he had his own bedroom. He imagined having money for a tutor in math. He imagined being wealthy enough to hire a bully to bully big-shot Eli. As he inhaled the exhaust of cars and buses, Pinny pictured being honored by Mars, Incorporated for selling his millionth Snickers. In his dream he saw the CFO,[11] Reuben Gamoran, pinning a massive chocolate medal on his chest and saying, "Excuse me, Pinny, can I have a Krackel bar?" But in his daydream, Pinny realized that Mr. Gamoran would not be asking him for a bar of Hershey's chocolate. Yet there he was, repeatedly calling his name! "Pinny, Pinny, PINNY!"

The shouts tugged Pinny from his reverie. It was not the CFO who was calling him; it was indeed a customer. "Sorry," Pinny said while stifling a yawn. "I was just thinking about something. How can I help you?"

"Pinny, I'd like a Krackle bar please. Nice day, isn't it?" the man said as he held out a five dollar bill.

Pinny started. He recognized that voice, but he just couldn't place it. The person even looked vaguely familiar, but again, Pinny couldn't remember where he had seen this guy.

---

11   Chief financial officer.

And, Pinny added to his mental list of observations, *this fellow knows my name. How in the–*

Suddenly it hit him like a ton of bricks! *Hey! It's him! It's the mystery guy from yesterday! Does he expect me to say something to him? Does he know that I recognize him? How should I act?*

Pinny wavered for a moment and then decided that he would treat Mr. Mysteryman just like everyone else. "Here's your chocolate, sir. And this," Pinny said as he slid some bills and quarters toward Mr. Green, "is your change."

Instead of reaching for the money, the man smiled broadly and said, "Remember me? I'm Josh Green. I'm the one who has an office in that dilapidated building over there." He nodded in the building's direction. "You can keep the change. It's a token of my admiration for your daring to come and see me.

"I also wanted to tell you how impressed I am with your effort and persistence with this stand. You display such fine character, thanking every buyer and saying hello to those who pass you by without making a purchase. I'll bet you're a model student in school."

The word "school" instantly transformed Pinny's face. Before Green's eyes, Pinny's pleasant, calm face was replaced with the sad visage of an individual in pain. The memory of the day's events flooded Pinny's mind. In that moment, Pinny lost control, and the wave of frustration that had been put aside at the start of his sales came crashing down on him and leaking out of the corners of his eyes.

At first, Josh stood still, hoping that Pinny would regain control and turn off his tears from within. However, after a few minutes passed without any sign of the well running dry, Josh felt stuck. He wanted to walk away. He barely knew this kid and whatever the issue was, it wasn't his business. Even more, what could he do? Josh was sure that the boy would not be interested in assistance from a virtual stranger. Josh started walking away. Glancing over his shoulder after his first few steps, Green saw Pinny's head on his table, shoulders heaving.

Josh turned back.

"Hey, Pinny," Josh said gently, giving Pinny plenty of space, "can I help? Want me to call your parents? Help you get home? I've seen that you're very friendly with old Mr. Silver. His office is nearby. Should I get him to come and help you?"

Receiving no reply, Josh thought to call Pinny's home, but he didn't see any business cards on the table. Josh took out his cell phone and dialed a number.

"Hello, may I please speak to Mr. Silver? Thanks. Mr. Silver? Josh Green here. I am outside at the candy stand.... Yes, the boy Pinny. Well, I'm not sure why, but he's very upset and I thought if you could come.... Sure, one second."

Josh extended his phone toward Pinny. "Pinny? Mr. Silver wants to talk to you."

Pinny took the phone and, sniffling, said, "Hello?"

"Pinny?" Mr. Silver said. "Are you in trouble? Do you need help?"

Coughing out the last of his sobs, Pinny assured Mr. Silver that he was all right. "I'm upset about something that happened in school and..." Pinny's voice trailed off as he tried to hold back a new torrent of tears that was threatening to come.

"You know what?" Mr. Silver broke the moment of silence, "I could leave my office in a few minutes. Wait for me by your corner and we'll walk home together."

Mr. Silver's worried voice and quick offer motivated Pinny to find some strength. "Mr. Silver?" Pinny had found his voice again. "It's okay. I don't want to trouble you. I can get home myself. Thanks so much for your concern. I feel better already. I'll be fine."

Mr. Silver had one last comment. "Don't thank me. All I did was answer my phone. Thank my good friend, Josh, for thinking to call me. He's a good man, that Josh. I know because he's helped me a few times when I needed it. Well, see you later and don't hesitate to come on up to my office if you need something." With this offer, Mr. Silver ended the call.

Pinny returned the phone to Josh and began to pack up his wares. Josh saw that Pinny looked better, so he turned and began walking away.

"See you around, Pinny," he called out.

"Wait! Thanks for your help," Pinny said. "I'm sorry for crying and holding you up. And I'm sorry for entering your office yesterday."

"No problem. I was a kid once too. I know that some days are tough."

Somehow, the crying had made the day's events less sad. Pinny's heart felt a bit lighter. He continued closing up his store as he said with a sheepish grin, "I bet you never had a day as tough as mine!"

Josh scratched his chin for a moment and then dared Pinny. "Oh yeah? Try me."

After Mr. Silver's words of praise about Mr. Green, Pinny felt safe enough to accept Josh's challenge as they sat there in public. Pinny related the painful events of the day, trying hard to avoid displaying his emotions. As Josh sat there listening to the long narrative, he found it difficult not to cry himself. Pinny's day had indeed been very hard.

Pinny came home late again that night. Their conversation had continued even after a waving Mr. Silver passed them on his way home. However, this time Pinny was not worried about what his parents would say. Just talking about the events of the day and expressing his thoughts about his troubles had really given Pinny's spirits a boost. Releasing his pain had made his heart feel lighter. He even felt confident that he could face any punishment his parents might levy against him for his late arrival with nonchalance.

Chapter Four

CHAPTER FIVE

Brows furrowed, Mark Malone looked at the computer's weather map and then checked his watch. The satellite images of the heavy cloud cover indicated that the whole eastern seaboard was in for the big storm brewing offshore. Doppler radar showed that the storm was already dumping massive amounts of rain into the Atlantic and was rapidly heading toward the coast. Mark compiled the information from the MOS[12] data and prepared what he would tell the people of Baltimore on WBAL radio at 5:05 pm.

One of the greatest difficulties in being a meteorologist, or "weatherman," as his kids called him, was being proven a fool by nature in public. Ever since Cleveland Abbe founded the United States Weather Bureau in 1901, meteorologists have been in mad pursuit of attaining elusive perfection at weather prediction. Using incredible math skills and knowledge of physics allowed the scientists of the early twentieth century to attempt predictions that were not simply guesses. A breakthrough in weather forecasting came in 1950. A team of meteorologists used an ENIAC[13] digital computer to create a twenty-four-hour forecast. Of course, the computer was just a bit slow. It took nearly twenty-four hours to come up with that forecast each time! Now, with the GFS, or Global Forecast System, in place, accuracy was much more likely, although meteorologists still analyzed the information from other weather models in order to adjust their predictions.

Mark was not worried or hesitant to say the truth as he saw it. He planned on informing all of the people within the range of his voice to prepare for flooding and serious water damage. This storm was coming quick and would dump about four inches of rain in twenty-four hours.

Heavy rain and strong winds were a normal part of life on the East Coast, especially during hurricane season. With the seas rising due to melting ice in the Arctic, flooding had also become something to expect. Already, those seashore towns like Norfolk, Virginia; Riviera Beach, Maryland; and others had ceded miles of their land to the hungry waves of the Atlantic Ocean. Even Annapolis, the capital of

---

12 Model Output Statistics is a technique for transforming weather statistics into a forecast understandable to laymen.
13 The name of the first electronic computer.

Maryland and home of the United States Naval Academy, suffered from permanent property shrinkage due to the new water level in the Chesapeake Bay.

What worried Mark, who was comfortably ensconced in his dark purple "chill seat" with a cup of vanilla coffee, was an e-mail he had received from a new, young research meteorologist. This young man's e-mail contained a singular opinion of what the upcoming storm would bring, and if he was correct, someone needed to tell the governor to prepare for a state of emergency.

The young man had written: "My research, using many past models of similar weather patterns coupled with the current ocean temperatures, humidity, and evaporation rates due to the greenhouse effect, indicates that as many as twelve inches of rain will fall in the upcoming storm."

This young man billed himself as a research meteorologist studying global warming and climate change. The e-mail had been sent to the address that WBAL posted on its website as contact information. Clearly, it seemed like another doomsday predictor making a guess using a smattering of technical knowledge. If this guy was legit, Mark would contact his colleagues in high places and they would warn the government.

Mark really wanted to ignore the dire warning. He was not going to make himself an easy target for every amateur forecaster in Baltimore. He was not going to go out on a limb and let the wind of inaccuracy blow him away from his place of employment.

But…

The data made sense. Running some numbers and looking up some old dynamic models, Mark saw truth in this fellow's words. The logical thing would be for Mark to call one of the other meteorologists on the radio station's staff. Even though they were not on duty now, he could run his dilemma by them and see what they had to say.

However, Mark hesitated. He imagined what his reaction would be if he were the one at home receiving the call from his colleague.

> *"Hello, Mark?"*
> *"Yes, Bill, what's up?"*
> *"Mark, I need your advice. I received this e-mail predicting some real weather trouble. Do you think that I should pay attention to it?"*
> *"Ha-ha-ha! Thanks for the good laugh. Listen, I gotta go. I almost fell for it. I guess things are a bit slow today. Well, I'll see you later. I've got the next shift."*

Way too embarrassing. No way, Mark thought.

Suddenly, Mark had an idea.

CHAPTER SIX

Mark went back to his desk and keyed in his e-mail account password. Mark hated clutter. His office was sparsely decorated with useful items and ambiance-enhancing weather memorabilia, but it was devoid of the piles of unopened mail, unfiled memos, old coffee cups, and assortment of office supplies that littered the offices of so many of his peers. This habit, which often served to irritate his family and friends, enabled Mark to find anything he wanted without much effort—like the current e-mail. There it was, with the subject line marked URGENT! DANGEROUS WEATHER. The sender was someone named Josh Green.

Mark double-clicked the e-mail and reread its contents. Then he opened a new browser window in Google Chrome and typed in "Josh Green meteorologist." Immediately, about 22,300 results appeared. Clicking the most informative but least reliable one, Mark was directed to Wikipedia. What he read as he scrolled down the page was impressive.

According to Wikipedia, Josh Green was a twenty-five-year-old scientist who had already earned a reputation as a progressive and serious researcher dedicated to improving the quality and safety of life on a climatically altered Earth. While still a senior in high school, Josh had cofounded what is now affectionately called by friends and foes alike "COOL." This non-profit organization raises billions of dollars to develop lightweight, long-lasting materials that go by the commercial name of COOL, to be used in clothing. Their money also supports the relocation needs of the millions of people each year who need to find new homes because the land where they and their families lived—sometimes going back for generations—has become the new home for a variety of fish. The article indicated that Josh was no longer involved with the organization "by mutual agreement."

Josh also made significant contributions to the science of meteorology and the study of climate change. Most notable was Josh's development of the PRIME Scope. Curious about this, Mark clicked on the blue site link at the bottom of the web page. He found himself reading an article from the *New York Times*.

Young Teen Wins $50,000 in Google Science Fair

By L. B. Kanner

To those who meet Josh Green, he seems to be just a regular kid. He likes sports, pizza, and hanging out with his friends. Josh's friends even talk about the time he cut class just to shop on Black Friday. But this sixteen-year-old Maryland native's favorite activity is very unkid-like. Josh studies weather and climate change. His room at home is covered with ancient charts that would perplex the modern meteorologist, not to mention an anemometer, barograph, regular barometer, and other items that this reporter never even heard of.

Josh loves science in general and weather in specific. Green explained his passion, "When I was young, I lost my home and almost my life during a storm. I am determined to find a way to protect other kids from experiencing my trauma." Green was referring to the storm in 2042—the first of a series of major storms in the recent past to reshape the map due to higher sea levels.

The teen's prototype of what he calls a PRIME Scope has received worldwide plaudits. PRIME is an acronym for Pulse Radar Ice Melt Evaluator. The scope is able to calculate the melt rates of specific areas of ice and predict when it will completely change into water.

One potential use of the PRIME is to help scientists predict a precise date that a particular section of glacier will "calve" or break off from the main glacier. Currently, satellite monitoring enables glaciologists to see cracks that develop and lead to these ice breaks.

"Glaciers are constantly in motion," Noni Walkens, lead researcher of the Alfred Wegener Institute explained. "They have their own flow dynamics. The science of the calving of icebergs is largely unresearched."

Co-researcher Steve Humbart agrees, "The process is somewhat mysterious."

With the PRIME Scope, the mystery is closer to being understood. Now scientists will be able to measure and predict—even years in advance—when to expect calving.

Mr. Bob Watson, owner of Alaskan Cruise, explained one benefit of having advance notice about a calving. "Each year, tourists spend nice amounts of money cruising the Alaskan coast to see the beauty of the world's glaciers. This pleasure is not without risk. In the past ten years, there have been more than a dozen fatalities and a hundred injuries connected with this form of recreation. Sometimes a calving glacier creates waves so large that people are swept off of the decks of larger ships, while smaller vessels are capsized. These risks increase insurance costs, too. Advance notice will help us schedule trips at times when there will be no risk to crews or passengers."

"I see many other uses for this tool," said Dr. Perry Samsoff, chair of the Department of Atmospheric, Oceanic, and Space Sciences of the University of Michigan. "With teens as talented and as devoted to climate issues as Josh Green, I see hope for the planet's survival past the year 2150," Samsoff enthused.

Out of the other eighteen finalists, the judges awarded first place, a prize of $50,000, to Josh Green. IT giant Google has been running the fair since 2008. Many valuable innovations have resulted, including a nuclear fusion reactor built by then-teen Taylor Wilson, and Ciara Judge's work with diazotroph bacteria to boost crop yields.

Josh plans to use his winnings to help pay for his education.

Wow, this guy was smart. But was he good enough for Mark to go out on a limb in this kind of situation? Mark made a snap decision. He would rely on the report.

I've been wrong plenty of times before. I'll present the forecast as Josh sees it, but without alerting the governor. It would serve the governor right to lose a possible presidential bid for not listening to WBAL's weather report! Mark thought while wearing a smile.

"Hey, Mark," the shift's producer called, "you're on in seven minutes. You need to hustle!" Noticing Mark's smile, he asked, "What's so funny?"

"I was imagining the headlines next November! 'Governor Loses Elections because of WBAL!'"

"Wha-a-t?"

"Uh, never mind," Mark replied. "I'll be ready in time!"

A few minutes later Mark was standing in the studio, wearing his headset and microphone. He heard the news anchorman say, "And now for the WBAL weather, we turn to our expert meteorologist, Mark Malone. So, Mark, the skies are black and big drops of rain are rapidly filling the reservoirs. What can we expect?"

"I hate to tell you, Ron, but you should get out your rowboat! This hurricane will likely be worse than Sandy and Katrina were—combined!" Mark began. "I urge everyone to take this storm seriously. I encourage people living in the coastal areas to…"

CHAPTER SEVEN

In the Maryland State House, there was a feeling of urgency in the air. The halls were filled with important-looking officials walking swiftly to and fro, carrying folders, files, or attachés. In their muted conversations, one could hear recurring words that seemed to sound to the beat of the heavy rains drumming on the stained glass windows. "Flood," "danger," "elections," "angry." Over and over they sounded. Flooding in many areas throughout the state had become severe in a short period of time. Even those entrenched in the State House on Capital

Circle were not safe from the creeping water. Already, there was flood water inching up Francis Street and Cornhill Street.

In the Office of Emergency Operations, the OEO, Governor Almond and the members of his emergency management team were gathered around a desk, listening to the voice of a staffer explain over the speakerphone why he could not come to the State House despite the emergency situation. With static and dead air interrupting his narrative, the staffer related how he and another fellow decided to drive together. They planned to cross via the Spa Creek Drawbridge. Driving along Duke of Glouster Street, they were entranced by the sight of the tranquil creek rapidly turning into a raging river due to the pouring rain. There was heavy traffic approaching the bridge. Cars were inching along, their drivers willing their windshield wipers to operate at warp speed to grant visibility beyond the hood of their cars. Some drivers, simply unable to see well enough, had pulled to the side of the road, a risky place to be when visibility was poor. Other cars were sitting in the middle of the road in pools of water, clearly stalled and blocking the flow of traffic.

Finally, after a long trip of but a few miles, the staffers' heavy SUV arrived at the approach to the bridge. It looked like a parking lot. The only reason that their car had actually reached there was because everyone ahead of them had eventually made a U-turn, hoping to find an alternate route. The traffic on the bridge was at a standstill.

"We could see that the cars on the deck of the bridge were already partially submerged in water. We were trying to decide what to do next," the staffer explained, "when the wind started howling and we saw a powerful wave wash over the railing. Suddenly the bridgedecks came apart, casting tons of steel and concrete, together with the ten or twelve cars that had been stuck there, down into the waters below."

At this point, the staffer broke down. They could hear him sobbing. The shock of witnessing such loss of life in such a violent way had penetrated his soul.

The governor's face was scrunched up in pain; tears fought their way out of the corners of his eyes. Carl Almond was a sensitive fellow. It was his sense of connection with the common man that had won him the governorship. Now, in the face of this unfolding tragedy, his emotional display, while appreciated by his advisors, was not timely. In crisis, a strong, firm, and unemotional response was the tool that brought confidence and calm to the masses. Carl wiped his damp eyes with his finger and used the momentary pause to reconfigure his facial expression to portray determination and intense focus.

"Continue please," he urged gruffly.

His sobs subsiding, the staffer's voice was suddenly cut off.

"Hello? Hello?" the governor called out, hoping that the connection had not been lost. But it was in vain. Either the staffer's cell had died or the storm was interfering with the signal.

The governor turned to Adjutant-General James Collins. "General Collins? What can we do from here?"

"Well, sir, we have mobilized the 183rd Field Brigade and the 44th Military Police Brigade of the National Guard. These units contain 5,000 troops trained in local weather disasters. In addition, we have called on my old unit, the 163rd Airlift Wing to work rescue. The challenge is that the winds are so severe that flying anything in this weather is nearly impossible. As soon as I heard about the bridge, I called upon the Navy to assist with the rescue of the bridge victims. Their divers are already actively involved in the rescue operations. We have also issued an alert through the media and over the Internet that everyone should remain inside, and we have opened emergency rescue phone lines—though we don't know how much good they will do and for how long they will last in this weather."

Chapter Seven   49

The general continued his report, his expertise in planning and superb organization showing with each detail he expounded. The State of Maryland was in good hands with Adjutant-General Collins at the helm of the OEO. This was not his first or second weather disaster. During his tenure, James Collins had dealt with many storms that flooded the streets, chemical spills that threatened to contaminate the water supply, and forest fires. Collins handled each situation to the best of his ability. He did occasionally make mistakes, but always moved forward using the lessons these mistakes had taught him and creating a better plan for "the next time." Adjutant-General Collins had the situation under as much control as anyone could expect.

"Sir," Collins continued, "this is what we're doing as we speak. However, I need to plan our next step. I am ready for your orders."

The governor scratched his balding head. "I need to know what the forecasters are predicting. Is this the worst? Can we begin to discuss cleanup and recovery yet?"

Allen Parker, OEO Chief, barked some orders to a staffer standing on his left. The staffer rushed out and returned a minute later holding a clutch of papers. He handed them to his boss. "Here, sir, are the latest reports on the weather. They are transcripts from the top weathermen in our area." Parker gave the ream of paper to his boss, the governor.

Governor Almond took the papers and began to rifle through them. He saw that the reports were from three separate meteorologists. He noticed that the storm had been given a name: Atlantis. As he read the papers, the governor automatically began humming the "Thinking Tune" for which he was famous. Two years earlier, when asked a tough question by reporters, the normally well-spoken governor had slipped into his hum. It was an instant hit! Radio stations began to play the audio of the governor humming as a way of introducing news or a conversation about him. People even began to use it themselves when thinking. The tune was such a good nonverbal reminder of the governor that he had even recorded himself humming it to use as a campaign advertisement! His humming continued, sometimes off-key, and finally concluded with a *hmm-hmm*.

Carl Almond spun toward the OEO chief. "Bah! These are useless! Mr. Parker, do these people actually call themselves meteorologists? Take a look here, here, and here!" The governor pointed to a place in each report with an emphatic jab. "These say that we'll get a maximum of four to five inches of rain. We exceeded that a while ago! And here! Just look at this rubbish—this utter nonsense! They must have used the *Farmer's Almanac*—of 1889, no less—to predict this... this...Atlantis!"

The governor read out loud for the benefit of all the team standing within earshot, "...will likely end in the early evening, leaving only minor damage in its wake..." Continuing with sarcasm he said, "And these guys spend four years in school to learn how to do this! *Hmph!* This isn't helpfu–"

Intimidated by the governor's strong outburst, the young staffer who had brought him the reports cleared his throat, interrupting the governor midsentence. "I know that the governor isn't fond of WBAL, but on my way in to the office today, I heard their top weatherman, Mark Malone, and he actually predicted this. Should I try to get ahold of his latest prediction?"

To say that the governor wasn't fond of WBAL was PC, politically correct. More precise would be to say that the governor despised WBAL. While running for the governorship for his first term, a disgruntled former employee from his company, Almond's Almond Processing plant had gone to the FBI with the accusation that the AAP was involved in smuggling drugs in their shipments of almonds, as well as tax fraud. This led to an investigation that almost cost Carl Almond the election, despite being cleared of any wrongdoing. Someone in the upper management at WBAL had decided to use the radio station to publicly eviscerate AAP, and Carl Almond in particular, as an example of corrupt politics in Maryland. Even when the story was no longer newsworthy, WBAL talk show hosts still reminded their listeners of what Almond had been accused. So, it was quite understandable that WBAL's weather report was not originally brought to the governor's attention.

Desperate for any accurate news, Carl replied to the staffer with a curt nod of the head, "Get it. Get it fast!"

CHAPTER EIGHT

Minutes later, Malone's forecast was in the governor's hands. As he read through it, his head bobbed up and down like the bobble-head that would one day (if he won the election again) be in his likeness. "This is more like it! See? He's predicting more than fifteen inches of rain in many areas. There is even a warning of bridge trouble, and the Spa Creek Bridge is cited by name! We need to speak with this fellow and have his input about how to proceed."

The timid staffer asked, "Should I try contacting the radio station, sir?"

OEO Chief Parker raised his right hand slightly, a gesture indicating that he wanted to say something before the governor responded. "Sir, I think that it's important that he come here and take part in our meetings in person."

Almond was skeptical. "We have to be realistic now. He would have to find a way to drive here that wasn't flooded. I think it would be better if we set up a Skype conference." Turning to his staffer, he continued, "Billy, call his station and see what you can do."

Billy left the room. He headed toward the communications center within the State House. Although there were phones all over the mansion, the people working in the CC, as it was called, seemed to know how to reach the unreachables. Billy wanted to insure that his mission would succeed.

"Hey there, Ears," Billy called out as he entered the very large and cold room of the CC. "The Big Fellow wants you to contact Mark Malone from WBAL to set up a video conference. Can you do it?"

"Are you doubting my dot-com abilities, Billy? I should have him on the screen before you learn how to tie your shoelaces!"

Billy and "Ears," as the head of the CC room was called, were friends from college. Ears had majored in communications and Billy in political science. Now Ears was enjoying a successful career in the State House, and Billy was pandering to various high-ranking politicos with the hopes of becoming someone mentioned in the well-studied book, *The History of the United States*.

Billy waited as Ears got down to business. His gaze swept around the room. Billy could not understand why, since the advent of the mini-microchip, the room still had so many big machines whirring and beeping with their lights flashing. He also never understood why the air conditioner was turned up to full blast when it was cold outside. As Billy pulled his sweater around himself tightly, he thought, *this room is freezing!*

"Billy," Ears called out to him after a few minutes, yanking him out of his reverie, "I can't do it. Phone wires are down all over the place. Winds are up to seventy-five miles per hour! No way. Even the e-mail isn't working. The storm is wreaking havoc on all electronic communication!"

"Well, Ears, thanks for trying. Now I get to be the guy who delivers the bad news to the big cheese. Oh-h, why did I come in today?" Billy let out a groan that was half in jest, but half serious.

Ears laughed. "Isn't that why you spent $200K at the University of Maryland? So you could be some big politician's lackey?"

Billy trudged back to the governor's office. Somberly, he reported his failure to contact the radio station. "But, sir," he continued, hoping to one day accompany Governor Almond to the White House, "maybe the National Guard could pick up this Malone by helicopter."

Carl Almond was feeling a bit desperate. Any idea was welcome. "General?" he said.

General Collins had been speaking with some of his men about all the problems this storm and its aftermath would cause. Now hearing the governor call him, the general excused himself with a salute and walked across the expansive room to Almond. "Yes?"

Almond explained about what had happened with the meteorologists and he described the failed attempt to contact Mr. Malone. "So, my staffer, uh..."

"Billy," Billy inserted for the governor.

"Right. Billy had this interesting idea about having you send someone to get him by air, using the Guard. Can this be done safely?"

The general thought for a minute or two before replying. "I am willing to give the command to my personal pilot. I trust him and I am confident that if he feels the situation is unsafe, he will not hesitate to abort the mission. I will make it quite clear that he is not to endanger his life in any way."

Chapter Eight

However," continued Collins, "if you did not arrange with the forecaster to be picked up, maybe he won't agree to come. What should my pilot do if Mr. Malone refuses to fly to Annapolis?"

"Then arrest him for endangering the public," Almond replied sharply. "I can't solve every problem, General. Have your man get creative and bring me this guy!"

Unaffected by the governor's harsh tone, Collins nodded and said, "I'll get on it right away." He turned on his heel and headed to the cafeteria, where he would find his helicopter pilot. Collins had worked for many high-ranking military men who had to operate under pressure. The governor's reactions matched the best of them in a tough spot.

❖

The governor sat down on the plush brown couch that had graced the Emergency Operations Office since 1999. Almond had spent many nights sleeping on this couch—not even purposely! It was extremely comfortable. Alone in the room, he reached toward the small antique end table next to the right armrest and lifted a bottle of beer that was chilling in a bowl of ice for just this kind of situation. Already, reports of extensive damage to the roads, electricity, railway lines, and personal property had passed through his hands. For whatever it was worth, Almond had already declared a state of emergency. But until he knew what the worst would be, there was nothing else he could do.

"Excuse me, Governor?" his assistant interrupted.

"Yes, Billy?"

"They told me to tell you that there are reporters who've been gathered in the pressroom for well over an hour already who are demanding to question you!"

The governor made a nasty face, kind of what kids do when their teacher announces a test in math. "All right. I'm coming."

After Billy withdrew, the governor wearily headed for the door. He paused in front of the full-length mirror that was strategically mounted on its inside. It served to alert the governor as to how he was looking before he left the room. Seeing his reflection enabled him to paste his famous "upbeat-even-in-a-crisis" look on his face.

Now, he straightened his yellow, smiley-face necktie, tucked his shirt into his pants, and massaged his cheeks until a true smile appeared on his face. His efforts paid off; he was looking much better. Straightening his hunched back, the governor walked out of the room with the air of confidence he had practiced so often.

CHAPTER NINE

"Sir! You look so calm and collected! I'm from WPIK, Pikesville. I was wondering if I could get a few questions answered while we walk?"

The reporter accosting the governor as he left the OEO office was a young kid, barely in his twenties, dressed in a dark blue suit with a loud purple shirt poking through at the lapels and bottoms of his jacket sleeves. His hair had enough gel in it to supply a band of rock stars. He was wearing a pair of high-tech Google Glasses that would serve to record both the audio and video of the interview. This left his right hand free to shake the unenthusiastic governor's hand and simultaneously pat his left hand on the governor's back in a friendly way.

How did he get past security? thought the governor. *Is this guy really a reporter?*

After what seemed like ten minutes, but was really about a minute, a security guard ran up to disentangle the reporter from the governor. "You are under arrest! You crossed the rope marking this area as restricted. Face the wall and spread your hands and feet!"

The governor made a quick decision. If this reporter was arrested, even though it was within the bounds of the law, there would be yet another member of the media against him as he pursued his presidential bid. It was tough enough contending with WBAL while he sought the highest office in the land; creating more media bitterness would make his battle to the top even harder.

I need to use this situation to my advantage, Almond thought. He addressed the guard politely, "Would you mind leaving us for a moment? I'd like to speak to him for a bit." The guard let him go and walked back to his post.

"What's your name, young man?" the governor asked, his voice taking on a tone of camaraderie.

"Steve Drescol from WPIK, sir." His words rushed out at the speed of a locomotive. Drescol continued without as much as a pause for a breath. "It is a great honor and also a surprise that you are treating me so kindly. You see, I'm new to the reporting scene and my boss gives me all the tough assignments—the ones that nobody else wants. If I make things work and get the story despite the difficulties, then I might be made into a regular reporter! My editor told me to cover the storm here in the State House because 'the newbie gets the toughest jobs and the governor is an ogre with the media' to quote my *superior*." Steve paused upon concluding with this sarcastic reference to his boss.

Extending his hand enthusiastically this time, the governor said, "Steve, I am Carl Almond, governor of Maryland and hopefully the future 57th president of the United States! A pleasure to meet you. Look, there are many reporters waiting for me. But I like your honesty and your stick-to-it attitude, despite having a difficult boss. I want to help you out. So what do you say if after the storm is over and we finish helping everyone get their lives back to normal, we meet for a private interview, hmm?"

"Awesome!" chuckled Steve.

"Now, though, I must feed the sharks waiting to devour me! Come."

The governor walked with Steve and one of his security details toward the pressroom. Steve entered in the rear, like all the other members of the press, and the governor continued on to the entrance by the podium. He walked in and up to the lectern, behind which was a heavy curtain sewn to look like the state flag: gold and black squares on the first and fourth quarters—representing the colors of the Calvert family, Lords of Baltimore, and the other two quarters bearing the arms of the Crossland family. Looking around the room, his eyes barely took in the ornate walnut woodwork that accented the walls. Nor did he think about the gilded ceiling with its magnificent fresco that was suspended twenty feet above his head. He noted the paltry number of reporters. The normally full room now held only eight. Clearly, the storm had prevented others from joining them.

"Welcome. I'm glad you were able to make it despite the ferocity of Atlantis. Although I would prefer to have others with me from the OEO, this is a very busy time and everyone needs to do their jobs. It was agreed that I would answer what I can now, and we will hold another press conference later for the questions I can't answer.

"I just would like to make sure that you share with your readers and listeners that our emergency management team is working very hard to contain the chaos from the storm as much as possible. At this moment, we are bringing a leading meteorologist here to give us the latest information about what to expect for the next twenty-four hours. Now, let's get to your questions."

The reporters began to call them out all at once, making answering just one question impossible. The governor suggested, "We have only a small crowd. Let's just take turns."

"Sir? Do you know the current death toll from the storm?"

"General Collins has reported that as of 4:00 pm today we know of thirty-five deaths in our state and at least the same in the New York/New Jersey area. Obviously, we do not know much about the areas inaccessible due to flooding."

"Mr. Governor, how many troops from the National Guard have been called out?"

"Five thousand troops on the ground plus two hundred men and women for air rescue."

"Sir, Benji Smith from WBAL here. I heard that you ridiculed the weather reports from most of the meteorologists in the state. You called them incompetent. Can you explain why you were so critical of the people who are working at this very moment under intense pressure to keep the citizens of Maryland safe?"

The governor's face started turning red. In a voice that displayed controlled anger, he answered, "I do not care to dignify gossip. We are here to talk about the emergency and that is all. If you are looking for what to post in the social media, you'll have to speak to someone else."

An awkward silence followed for half a second.

"Governor? What about the flooding of government buildings? Is there any plan to put up sand bags around them or to move the electronic equipment?"

Chapter Nine

"Actually, the National Guard, together with volunteer groups like Habitat for America and Eagle Scouts United, *are* putting sandbags where it is feasible, but there is so much rain, and incredible wind gusts of up to ninety miles per hour, and downed trees and electric lines, all making any movement outside difficult and dangerous."

"Do we know what was the highest storm surge in the state so far?[14] Where was it and what kind of damage did it cause?"

"It seems that Atlantic City and downtown Baltimore had surges greater than nine feet above normal tide levels. As for the damage, I can only say that the images I saw are horrific. I expect that local damage will be in the billions of dollars."

From behind the heavy curtain, Billy poked out his head and called in a stage whisper, "Governor, that Mark guy is here!"

The governor nodded his head, acknowledging the update, while facing the reporters. He was not planning to say anything more to them about the visitor who was about to become an integral member of the OEO team. Maybe later, after a strategy was worked out, there would be latitude to give them more.

"At this point," the governor said in a heavy tone, "we have many details that we need to work out, so I need to go. I hope that in a few hours we will see the storm calm down and the recovery process begin. Perhaps we can reconvene in three hours. Thanks for your time."

As the reporters put away their equipment and chatted, the governor left the room. Had he turned around, he would have seen Steve Drescol following closely behind. Even the security guard overlooked Steve's trailing the governor, and Steve miraculously squeezed himself into the OEO just as the office door was shutting on what was to be an important meeting.

---

14 Water height the rivers and oceans reached above their usual levels due to a storm.

CHAPTER TEN

Mark Malone was standing as the governor entered. He was wearing yesterday's clothes. His slacks and sport coat were massively wrinkled. They looked like they'd been slept in, which was the truth. His white shirt had coffee stains on it. And a tie? He had abandoned it the moment he finished reading Josh's predictions. Mark did not look like a person who deserved respect. Mark did not, at least in his current state, give the impression that he was *the* person to save the state in any way.

Mark knew this and had tried to tell the soldier who had picked him up—almost literally—from the radio station that he needed to change before leaving. But the fellow just wasn't interested.

As the governor entered the room with his arm extended and his voice issuing a warm greeting, Mark tried to explain his awful appearance. "I'm sorry that I look so disheveled, but…"

The governor cut him off mid-sentence. "Never mind. Look, the important thing is that you're here and can help us. The fact that you came shows you are willing to work with me. I appreciate that very much!"

Mark bristled at the governor's presumptuousness. "Actually, my arrival could be called a kidnapping! I never agreed to come. I was forced to come by a soldier wearing a gun. I admit that I didn't argue with him as much as I could have, but I was still forced. As you know, I work for WBAL and they have indicated to us that if we openly side with you on anything, our jobs will be in peril. So I don't think that I *will* help you out."

The governor's face turned red for the second time in an hour. His words, uttered slowly and calmly, were sharp and stinging. "Are all you newspeople the same? What exactly is important to you? Just yourself? Or are you interested in helping the people of Maryland? You know as well as I do that if you hadn't wanted to come, you wouldn't have. So stop wasting time and let's agree that you are not helping *me*. You are helping the people of Maryland! Okay?"

Now Mark's face colored. However, his red face was not one of anger, but of embarrassment. He realized that the governor was right. The truth was that when the helicopter with the National Guard logo had landed in the parking lot off the entrance to the radio station, everyone was excited and wondering what the reason was for such a special visit. The pilot entered the reception area, where some of the staff had already gathered. After requesting to see Mark, he had been summoned there from his office.

The pilot explained to him what was being asked of him. Mark loudly protested the idea of leaving the station and joining the governor. But the real reason for his protest was not an expression of his political preferences. This was a performance mostly for his superiors, so they would think that he was acting in accordance with their preferences.

The governor was right. Truthfully, Mark had wanted to come. He wanted to help the people of the state. He didn't even mind helping the governor if it didn't cost him his job. Of course, pride would not permit Mark to admit as such.

"Fine. I'll help," Mark said, attempting to put a begrudging tone in his voice. "What do you need?"

"As you heard when you were picked up," the governor explained, "we need to get a grip on the weather forecast: to know who will suffer the brunt of Atlantis' fury and when the storm will pass, so we can begin assessing the damage, and draw up a rescue and repair strategy. I read a number of meteorologic reports and found that yours was astonishingly accurate. I thought you would be very valuable to our team in properly evaluating the situation."

Mark always thought of himself as humble. If not exactly humble, at least not prideful. But his self-image was suddenly challenged. Mark knew he had not predicted the weather; it was that other guy, Josh Something-or-other who had gotten it right! Really, he should say, "I appreciate your confidence in my abilities, sir, but the truth is that I got my information from someone else." Yet, to admit that now and look bad in front of the entire emergency management team, especially after the governor had invested so much into getting him here, was unthinkable to him. Even worse, Mark tried justifying to himself why telling the governor about Josh would be a bad idea! But he couldn't come up with anything reasonable. In his heart, he knew that he was simply basking in the respect he was being shown and that he was too cowardly to embarrass himself. But deep in his soul, his moral compass kept telling him to tell the governor about Josh.

"Mark?" the governor said after a minute, "Can we get to work?"

"Uh...okay." Mark had made his choice. "Look at my screen here," he said as he powered up his laptop. "The different colors on these maps will help us get a clear picture of current and future storm activity."

CHAPTER ELEVEN

"GO-O-O-D AFTERNOOON, Maryland! It's 4:07 pm on this sunny Tuesday. You are listening to our show, Talk About It, with your favorite host, Rick Edell. If you would like to share your worldy wisdom with everyone, call us at 877-439-TALK! We have two lines available. Let's talk now with Arnold from Cecil County. Arnold?"
"Yes. Rick?"
"Go ahead, Arnold. You are on the radio with Rick Edell from WPIK, the station to pick for the best listening."

"Rick? I just wanted to say that the governor did a great job handling the storm. He is just the guy we need to be the next president. If he could handle Super-Storm Atlantis, he could certainly handle the Russians, the Arab terrorists, anyone. You know what I mean?"

"I certainly do, Arnold. Actually, you just gave me a great segue into a special report from the newsroom. Let's go there now. Tom?"

"Thanks so much, Rick. WPIK is Maryland's radio station known for reporting the latest in news first. So here's Steve Drescoll with a special bulletin."

"Steve Drescoll here from WPIK. I'm standing outside the State House, where I just finished an exclusive post-storm interview with Governor Carl Almond. I see why the voters polled by UMBC[15] gave him such high marks on his handling of the most recent super-storm to hit Maryland. At 75 percent popularity, Governor Almond enjoys a strong support that may win him office space in the White House in the upcoming elections. During the interview, Almond did not hesitate even once, thus depriving me of the pleasure of hearing his 'Thinking Tune' firsthand. Clearly, he already knew what he wanted to say and said it beautifully.

"First, the governor extended his condolences to the families of the fifty people who died in the storm, most of them perishing when the Spa Creek Bridge was torn apart by a massive wave. He also noted that the cost of the storm has not been fully determined, but as of now exceeds $150 billion.

"Quoting OEO Chief Allen Parker, Almond told me that the estimated damage to Maryland's shores is serious. Besides the

---

15 University of Maryland, Baltimore County.

piers and harbors that need to be rebuilt, and beaches that have been swept away, the water level is now another foot higher on the land at low tide, ceding more land to the ocean. "The governor also praised the entire team at the OEO and the National Guard for their immediate and efficient action in preventing even more deaths and damage throughout the state and conducting a major rescue effort. In addition, he announced that he will be bestowing the Order of the White Oak—the highest civilian honor that a governor can give—on Mark Malone of WBAL for his singular, accurate weather reporting and his work with the OEO."

Josh flicked off the radio. He had heard enough. He just sat in his chair in his office on Northern Parkway, frowning. Josh was upset. He did not mind that he was not receiving an award for forecasting. But he *was* frustrated by the fact that Mark had accepted all the credit and, clearly, had given him none. The governor had no idea that Josh existed and the role he had played in helping Maryland.

This thought made Josh very sad. Much of the money supporting his work on global warming and climate change came from grants, and with many of the grants that were available, a letter from an important political figure praising all the abilities and accomplishments of the person applying for the money would really help.

Josh was personally running out of money. His historic accomplishments in inventing the PRIME Scope and cofounding the COOL group displayed his expertise in science, but the fact that he currently had no cash left from either project served as a testament to Green's lousy business acumen. His current source of income—at least for now—was his salary as an assistant professor of atmospheric science in UMBC. Although it seemed like he did most of the work and the full professor just took it easy, Josh's salary was only $55,000, while the professor earned $90,000. His $55K was enough to live on, but not enough to enable him to follow his passion: climate stability. Now Josh would need to beg, borrow, and who-knows-what to get the funds to continue to study and develop realistic solutions to the effects of climate change.

Josh decided to put the whole thing out of his mind. One lesson that life had taught him over and over is that if something's out of your control, there's nothing to be gained by stewing about it. Josh had no power over the situation. He was not going to e-mail Mark about his "oversight," nor e-mail the governor to claim credit for his forecasts out of the blue. *I might as well let the matter drop and prepare for tomorrow's lecture*, he thought.

So, Josh began preparing. An hour passed. Josh only came up with one paragraph of notes. His mind kept pulling him back to his frustrations about Atlantis. Josh stood up to get some coffee. The extra caffeine sometimes put him in a good mood.

Josh took the hot drink back to his desk. As he was setting it down, the bottom of his UMBC mug hit his stapler and the mug overturned. The scalding drink simultaneously splashed all over the front of his clothes and his notes.

"OUCH-H!" Then Josh lost it. In addition to feeling depressed about Mark claiming all the credit for his work, Josh usually felt down after a severe storm. This time though, there was another reason on top of the others. During the storm, his car had been parked in a low-lying garage and was thoroughly covered by water, destroying his $20,000 investment. Josh's inquiries to his insurance company proved futile. They adamantly answered him, "We're sorry, sir, but your policy did not cover damage due to acts of G-d."

Now that his shirt and pants and valuable notes were stained and his skin was scalded, Josh broke down and began to cry. His sobs overrode the sound of his fire door being pulled open.

Pinny stood in the doorway and beheld a foreign sight. An adult was crying like a baby!

"Josh?" Pinny called in a timid voice as he approached the middle of the room.

"Josh, it's Pinny. What's wrong? Can I help? Please stop crying." Reaching the desk, Pinny put his arm across Josh's shoulders.

Pinny desperately wanted to know why an adult, especially like Josh, who looked at life so positively, would cry. What could possibly be *so* bad for him? But Pinny had been raised with *derech eretz*. Asking adults such personal questions was inappropriate. So he didn't ask. But his face betrayed his thoughts.

"Pinny, I know you want some answers. Maybe I'll explain what made me so sad another time. But now, let's get busy. You promised to help me review my forecast and match it against what actually happened during Super-Storm Atlantis. Look at this screen." Josh led Pinny to a computer on the far left side of the desk. Pulling up a brown folding chair, Josh indicated that Pinny should sit down.

"This contains all of the information relating to my predictions about the storm. Now I'll go to my computer." Josh turned to the computer that was sitting on a computer table at a right angle to the desk and sat down in front of it. "I'm going to read off my screen the statistics from the impact infograph posted on www.livescience.com of what actually happened during the storm, and we will see how they match up to each other."

Josh began reading the information. "Okay. First look at the place marked 'Flooding.' That's what I predicted would be the amount of water coming from the ocean onto the land. On my chart it's called 'Inundation.' Baltimore's Inner Harbor area, five feet of water reaching inland about three-quarters of a mile. Was that what I predicted?"

Chapter Eleven

Pinny took a minute to locate the information on his screen. "You have here '4+ feet, a half mile.' Sounds pretty close to me. You know what? I'll read what you've got here and you just give me a thumbs-up if your prediction was within a foot deep and a quarter mile into land of what actually happened. If it's more off than that, give me a thumbs-down and I'll make a note of it so you can check it out later."

Josh smiled broadly. "Sounds good!"

Pinny looked at his screen. "You had pegged Annapolis, six feet, about a half mile."

Josh gave a thumbs-up.

"Wow! That almost reached the State House!" Pinny exclaimed.

As they worked together, with Josh's predictions being mostly accurate a feeling of excitement for his friend's success swelled within him. Pinny felt true pleasure watching the smile on Josh's face flash each time he was correct.

Of course, Pinny was also thrilled to be participating in this really cool study. He anticipated telling some of his friends in school about it. Every student knows that science labs are fun, but here Pinny was being a real scientist—well, a scientist's assistant anyway! Pinny was not the most popular boy in school, being relatively quiet and reserved, and he knew that when they heard about his important "job," some of his classmates would be impressed and have greater respect for him. *Maybe*, Pinny thought, *I will become more of a person and not just part of the group.*

When they finished with the water levels, they moved on to wind speed matching, and then to temperature comparisons. Upon concluding each category, Josh would break out in a little impromptu song and dance. He would sing, "Yay, we did it; we did what's good; we predicted the weather as a good meteorologist should!" to some made-up tune. At some point Pinny suggested that they sing "*Siman Tov u'Mazel Tov.*"

"What's that?" Josh asked.

"It's a song Jews sing when they are celebrating a success, whether it's a wedding, a birth, a new job, completing a section in study—anything!" Pinny declared.

"Cool!" Josh said thoughtfully. "You know, I'm Jewish. I don't know much about Judaism, but I think it'd be awesome to learn a Hebrew song! It'd probably be much better than the one I made up here today!" That is how Josh and Pinny found themselves abandoning their work for twenty minutes for a brief music break.

After about another two hours of work and a little play, Josh and Pinny shut down the computers and prepared to leave Josh's office. As Pinny closed the lights and headed out the fire door, Josh let out a big sigh. "Pinny," he said, "I really enjoyed having you around. Being a part-time climate guy is kind of lonely, but you really made today end on an upbeat note."

CHAPTER TWELVE

Walking into school the next day, Pinny had a spring in his step and a smile on his lips. He felt good about himself. He felt important for helping Josh, and that translated to an overall positive self-image. Each person he passed received an enthusiastic greeting of "Good morning!" Even the janitor noticed a difference. "Hey, Tony," Pinny exclaimed as they passed each other in the hallway, "have a great day!" Tony grinned and shook his head in wonder.

Pinny continued into his classroom. The cacophony of noise that emanated from the room would have deafened a herd of elephants. The twenty-five boys there all seemed to be talking at the same time. And mostly, they were discussing the storm.

"My uncle had flooding in his second floor bedroom! The water got into all his shoes that were on the floor and…"

"Our power was out for almost a week and we used candles when we went to bed…"

"Well, *we* just went to our cousin's house and…"

"I heard that a bridge was destroyed!"

"We were lucky! Two years ago we lost power for a month, so my parents bought a generator. We ended up being the only house on our block with electricity!"

All the talkers just kept on talking when the *rebbi* came into the room. The *rebbi* set up his materials for the day. He placed his Gemara on his shtender and his *Chumash* and *Navi* on the desk. He took his roll book out of his dark red, hard-shell briefcase and looked around the room, taking attendance.

During all this, the shmoozing continued. Nobody paid any attention to the salt-and-pepper bearded man moving about in the front of the room.

Back at his desk, Rabbi Fishoff connected his smartboard to his laptop and opened the presentation that he had prepared for the day's lesson. Ready to begin, the *rebbi* stood in front of his *shtender* and said, "*Rabbosai?*"

This single word uttered at a normal volume had the same effect as an alarm going off. The boys raced to their desks, sat down, and opened their Gemaras. Such classroom control came out of the students' respect and love for the *rebbi*. Rabbi Fishoff was known as a tough educator with an old-school approach to *chinuch*. If he had a discipline issue in class—a boy shmoozing, reading a book at his desk, making funny faces, or the like—it lasted all of a minute. The perpetrator would see his *rebbi* bring an extra chair over to him and sit down. He would hear the melodious tune of the Gemara from Rabbi Fishoff's lips. He would smell the strong coffee fragrance that radiated from *rebbi's* long, graying beard. Finally, the *teshuvah*-filled student would feel his *rebbi's* heavy arm draped over his shoulder, pulling him in a back-and-forth sway to the words of the Gemara. Thus, without uttering a word, all twenty-five boys were focused again and learning.

Rabbi Fishoff was not just successful with his students in the classroom. During recess and lunch, it was typical to see Rabbi Fishoff having an animated discussion with a student about the Ravens' chances at the Super Bowl or assisting a boy with his math homework that was due that day.

Now, as he started the topic of *Shomer sheMasar leShomer*, Rabbi Fishoff looked into the eyes of each *talmid*, one by one. The smile on his face was contagious, and when the *rebbi's* gaze reached a boy who was not already doing so, the boy broke into a smile. When his eyes reached the seat in the far back corner, they rested on Pinny's face. Rabbi Fishoff paused for an extra moment. Pinny was generally a reserved child. Even when he smiled, it was only a skin-deep kind of smile. Yet today, Pinny had a genuine smile on his face. There was even a twinkle in his eyes.

"Pinny," Rabbi Fishoff said, affording Pinny the honor of special attention, "how are you this morning?"

"*Baruch Hashem* fine, Rebbi."

"Pinny, did your family suffer any damage during the storm?" his *rebbi* asked, making small talk.

"No, Rebbi," Pinny answered.

As Pinny responded, Rabbi Fishoff noticed that the mention of the storm seemed to delight him. "Did something special happen to you during the storm?"

Pinny struggled with what to say. On the one hand, he wanted to tell his friends all about Josh and the predictions. On the other hand, he was a little afraid that the class would view him as a nerd. Finally, Pinny replied, "Well, I got to spend some time with a real meteorologist because of the storm, and that was really special to me."

"Wow, that is special. I want to hear all about it! How about at recess today you tell me?" With these few words, Rabbi Fishoff had solved Pinny's concern. If the *rebbi* was interested and thought it was cool, then nobody could tease him!

The smile on Pinny's face grew bigger. "Sure, Rebbi, I would love that, if Rebbi has time."

"Beautiful! Okay, *Rabbosai*, now it's time to begin the new *sugya* of *Shomer sheMasar leShomer*."

CHAPTER THIRTEEN

Pinny paid extra attention to the *shiur* today. He was in a very upbeat mood before arriving at school, and now, with his *rebbi's* love filling his heart, Pinny felt a love for the Gemara growing within him. He did not even realize that he had raised his hand numerous times during class to answer questions and to clarify difficult points—something that Pinny was always reluctant to do in front of his classmates.

When recess finally came, Pinny found himself standing at the edge of the baseball field, sharing his experience with Josh not only with his *rebbi*, but also with most of his other classmates.

"So we saw how accurately he had predicted all those things!" Pinny said, concluding his "presentation."

"That is really incredible! You are very fortunate to have had such a fantastic adventure. Uh," Rabbi Fishoff said, pausing to look at his watch, "there are still a few minutes left to recess and I need to get some coffee." Rabbi Fishoff walked away, giving the boys a big smile and a wink.

The rest of the morning was equally pleasant for Pinny. He listened and participated. His *rebbi* was pleased and his classmates treated him respectfully.

The lunch bell ended the *Navi* class mid-sentence. Even Rabbi Fishoff would not stand between the boys and the delicious hot lunch that the yeshivah served.

The volume in the hallway increased as students poured out of their many classrooms. They had to pick their way around people, books, and knapsacks as they headed to the lunchroom.

As the boys lined up to receive their hot dogs and French fries, the conversation turned back to the storm. Some boys who were in line near Pinny began to ask him some details about Josh and his work.

"Is he Jewish?" Azriel asked Pinny.

"He's Jewish, but he doesn't know anything about Judaism. Actually, I taught him the song '*Siman Tov.*'"

Nesanel, the computer guy in the class, turned to Pinny. "Are his computers really advanced?" he asked.

"You bet! He has the most advanced! I saw one that said Intel 76! Those processors cost thousands of dollars! He has this program that links his computers to satellites. Obviously, he has a license for it, and I watched the storm in real time from above the earth! I felt like Avraham Avinu when Hashem took him outside so that he could count the stars!"

The line kept moving forward. Pinny's turn came. He loaded his red plastic lunch tray with two hot dogs in buns and a heaping portion of fries. He also grabbed a few packets of ketchup, a cup of juice, and a few napkins, and added them to his tray. Pinny scouted the tables reserved for his grade, thinking that he would sit with his friends.

Over there. I could sit down and eat at the table by the window with Nesanel and Avreimi, Pinny thought. *They were interested in what happened to me yesterday.* Pinny walked toward their table.

"WELL, LOOK WHO'S HERE," a voice boomed into Pinny's ear. "MY DEAREST *FRIEND*, PINNY!"

A shiver shot up Pinny's spine as he recognized the loud, taunting voice of Eli Truxenberg. Pinny realized that the great day he had been enjoying was about to end. Maybe, if he ignored him, Eli would vanish!

"HELLO-O! I'M TALKING TO YOU, WEATHERMAN!" Eli bellowed, peering into Pinny's face. He then reached out and took some fries from Pinny's plate and began to eat them.

"Please do not take my food," Pinny said quietly.

"Ahh! He talks!" Eli then grabbed one of Pinny's hot dogs out of its bun and stuffed the whole thing in his mouth.

Pinny got angry. All of his resolve to remain quiet oozed out of him. "LEAVE MY FOOD ALONE!" Pinny shouted as he abruptly turned to head to the closest exit. Eli reached over and swung his fists up underneath Pinny's tray, launching the remaining food into the air and knocking the cup of juice all over Pinny's shirt.

"I guess your weatherman friend would say, 'It's raining juice and dogs.' Ha-ha-ha!" Eli picked up one of the ketchup packets and squeezed it out on Pinny's head. "Looks like you got hit by the storm!" Eli strutted out of the dining room.

Pinny hung his head in shame. To be humiliated without fighting back was so embarrassing. Tears trickled from his eyes. Avreimi came over and whispered, "Come to our table, Pinny; I'll get you more food. Don't let a jerk like Eli get you down. He's just jealous!" Pinny allowed himself to be led to Avreimi's table, but refused to eat the new food that Avreimi brought him.

While he used napkins and wet paper towels to clean up Pinny's hair, Nesanel made a suggestion. "Pinny, after lunch, let's go complain to the *menahel*! We'll get Eli in trouble and you won't need to deal with him anymore!"

Pinny looked up at Nesanel. "Thanks for the offer, but you know that Eli has some friends who would love to beat me up, and not just because of Eli. If we tell the principal and Eli is expelled, they'll still come after me. I'm just going to avoid Eli the rest of the day and maybe he'll forget about me."

So Pinny spent the rest of lunchtime slinking around corners and hiding in the shadows in order to avoid being spotted by Eli Truxenberg. He even claimed that his stomach hurt—which it did, but from worry—in order to be in the nurse's room when all the students had free time later in the afternoon. This same excuse helped Pinny leave school an hour early, protecting him from the dangers of Eli at dismissal time.

Since nobody was home when he arrived, Pinny grabbed his candy and headed out, navigating both cars and pedestrians in order to get to his corner. He admitted to himself that the real reason he was going was that he was hoping to see Josh. He had so much he wanted to discuss with him.

"I hope he's there," he muttered to himself as he looked at the windows on the fourth floor to see if the lights were on. They were! "Yes!" Pinny shouted. A few people on the sidewalk looked askance at his outburst. "Sorry," he said, as he walked swiftly to the fire escape and began to run up the steps.

Pinny pulled open the fire door that led to what had become one of his favorite places. "Josh?" Pinny called as he entered.

Chapter Thirteen   81

"Come on in, buddy," Josh's faint voice came from behind a large box-like contraption. "You're early! Is everything all right?"

Pinny made his way to the back of the box. "One second. First you gotta tell me what is this...this...uh...thing."

Josh, who's head had been inside the box, pulled it back out and stood up straight. "This is a Stevenson screen. And before you ask what that is, I'll tell you! A Stevenson screen is, to quote Wikipedia, 'an enclosure to shield meteorological instruments against precipitation and direct heat radiation from outside sources, while still allowing air to circulate freely around them.'"

Switching the tone of his voice to the deep baritone of a newscaster, Josh gave a speech.

"Look inside this box. Here in the far left corner I've put a hygrometer. Invented by Johann Lambert in the mid-1700s, this instrument is often found in museum display cases to measure the humidity. On the right side is a barometer, invented in the 1600s by a man named Torricelli. It measures atmospheric pressure. In books about ocean travels of old, like in the book *Typhoon* by Joseph Conrad, the barometer's mercury falling was a prelude to a storm. In the center, we have a pyranometer. This disk-shaped instrument has a sensor at the top that collects data on solar radiation. I'm not sure if I will add anything else yet! Now you are super-educated in meteorological equipment. How was your day?"

Pinny was laughing. Josh's presentation was just hysterical! "That was great! My *rebbi* would have loved it!"

"Your who?" Josh asked.

"My Torah studies teacher. My *rebbi*. Actually that was one of the things I couldn't wait to tell you about! Today in class, for some strange reason, my *rebbi* asked me if I had anything special regarding Atlantis to relate, so I told him that I helped you and he asked me to share the details during recess, which I did, with lots of classmates standing around, and my *rebbi* was really impressed and it was just so great that he wanted to know all about it!" Pinny finished his long-winded, run-on sentence with a loud inhalation.

"That does sound exciting. I hope you made sure that I sounded educated and successful!" Josh replied jokingly.

Together, Josh and Pinny walked over to the small refrigerator in the corner of the room. Josh took out two cans of Pepsi and handed one to Pinny. Pinny sat down on a purple bean bag that was strategically placed near the fridge, and Josh sat opposite him in a bile green recliner. Josh had once explained his chair to Pinny as an expression of the color of the sky during a storm and the lack of cash in Josh's pockets so that he couldn't turn down the offer of a free recliner from an old acquaintance.

As they sipped their soda, a comfortable silence reigned. Each of the young men was caught up in his own thoughts and—at least for the moment—nobody was sharing.

CHAPTER FOURTEEN

"Pinny," Josh asked, breaking the stillness of the afternoon, "you said that your *rebbi* was *one* of the things you wanted to tell me about. What was the other?"

Pinny stared at his empty soda can. He wasn't sure if he should be speaking to Josh about his personal problems. Josh didn't share the same religious background and outlook as Pinny, so he probably wasn't the ideal adult to help him. But, it was so easy to talk to Josh, and he was smart and nice.

Another reason for Pinny's hesitation was because of his mother. She had made some trouble when she spoke to Pinny's father just the day before.

◆

"Aharon, I'm worried about the relationship that Pinny has with this man Josh. I mean, he's spending quite a few afternoons with him. I think we need to tell Pinny that he may not spend any more time with this Josh until we meet him and get to know him."

Pinny tried to placate his parents' worries. "But, Ma? Ta? Remember I told you what Mr. Silver had said about him? And Mr. Silver said something good to Tatty about him in shul the other day."

Pinny's father thought for a minute and then said, "Actually, Pinny, I forgot about that. Mr. Silver's words did make me feel a little more comfortable about your friendship. Still, I think what Mommy is saying is correct. We'd like you to meet him only in public for the time being. He hasn't done anything wrong, but it's better to be safe. How about you arrange for us to meet him?"

"But, Ta," Pinny had protested, "how do I do that?"

"Find out if he's Jewish," his father began.

"But he is!" Pinny answered excitedly.

"Perfect! Invite him for a Friday night meal. We'll get to know him, and hopefully your mother and I will feel comfortable about your friendship."

◆

Already Pinny had disobeyed his parents by coming to Josh's office today. But in his upset state of mind after what had happened in school, Pinny really had forgotten his parents' prohibition until now. Seeking Josh's advice would probably be a further violation of his parents' wishes. So he decided on what he thought would be the perfect solution. He would do what his parents wanted first and then ask for advice!

"Josh? I know that you aren't very familiar with Judaism, but I was wondering if you'd be interested in coming to my house for our Friday night Shabbos meal. You see, we eat a very fancy meal with everyone together, and my parents would love to meet you. What do you say?"

Pinny would have gone around in a few more circles trying to express the invitation clearly without sounding foolish, but Josh took advantage of Pinny's pause and replied with an enthusiastic yes. "Sure, I'd like to come. I too want to meet your family. I'm honored that you came here to invite me!"

Pinny realized that Josh thought the invitation was the second thing Pinny wanted to mention. It wasn't. "Actually, that invitation kind of just popped into my head. I really wanted to ask your advice about something. Remember that bully? Well, today, on what started out as one of the best days in school ever, he struck again and really embarrassed me." Pinny recounted the events of the day in great detail. Upon concluding, he said, "So I'm stuck. I can't go to the principal or my *rebbi*. I don't know what to do!"

Josh sat there for a minute. He then stood up and got himself another can of soda. "I think," he said slowly while popping open the can, "that you should tell your parents and see what they say. I mean, I'm honored that you asked me, but I also was bullied as a kid, and I don't think I handled it in the best way."

Pinny was puzzled. "One second. You were bullied when you were young?"

"Yup."

"And you dealt with it?"

"Yup," Josh answered again.

Pinny hazarded a guess. "Well, I would think that if your parents taught you how to deal with your bully, it would probably be good advice for me too. I'll bet your parents are really great because they raised someone as nice as you."

Josh's eyes started to fill with tears. "Pinny, the point is my parents didn't teach me how to deal with the bully. You see, by this time I was being raised by my grandparents and I felt I couldn't talk to them about this problem, so I just decided what to do myself."

"Your grandparents? What happened to your parents?"

Josh sighed deeply. "You see, my parents…ah…they…I'd rather not discuss this now. Just, those were the facts. I made my own choice about the bully, and I know now that it was foolish and wrong."

Pinny did not inquire further about Josh's parents. He saw that the subject had upset Josh. But he did beg and plead for Josh to share his counter-bully method. "Please? I won't do it myself! I am just so-o-o curious! What did he do and what did you do? Come on, ple-e-ase!"

"Okay, okay. But if you use my approach, I am sure you will get in trouble! So I am telling you a story that has a lesson about what you should *not* do!

"When I was in seventh grade," Josh began, "I was already quite a nerd. I was already enthralled by weather. This was because…well… anyway, I was living with my grandparents at the time. One day I came to school and I realized that everyone was avoiding me. Even kids who had been my friends in the past kind of slid out of my way when I walked down the hall.

"After a few days of this, things kind of exploded. Our science teacher told us to pair up with a friend to work on an experiment. Usually, I was a person that everyone wanted to partner with, since I got the best grades and I didn't mind doing all the work. But this time, nobody even looked at me. There were twenty-two kids in the class, and the one who was usually left out sat down to work alone rather than with me.

"My teacher sensed something was wrong. She asked the kid who was sitting alone to work with me, but he just ignored her and the teacher never forced the issue. I was really hurt. I was angry and upset too.

"On the way home from school, I walked up to one of my former friends—his name was John—and grabbed him by his backpack. 'John,' I said, my face in his face so he could see how furious I was, 'I'm not going to let you go until you tell me what's going on and why everyone is avoiding me.'

"John then told me that the kid who had made himself the boss of the school had told everyone that I was being raised by my grandparents because I was violent and out of control. He said even my parents couldn't handle me because they were wimps, so they sent me to be raised by my grandparents. The bully had told everyone that since I could explode at any time, they should stay clear of me. And my friends believed him! After being with them for two years without any outbursts, they suddenly became afraid! So I decided I would teach this guy, I think his name was Pedro, a lesson."

With this, Josh paused. "Pinny, I can't. My approach was wrong. Let's just leave it."

"Oh my goodness!" Pinny cried. "You can't stop now!"

"Huhh? Okay. The next day, I came to school with a plan in my head and anger in my heart. I waited until recess. During recess, Pedro always hung out with his friends, or maybe we should call them henchmen. When the bell rang to go back to class, his henchmen went in with the rest of the students, but Pedro liked to stay outside until he received a personal invitation from the teacher on duty when *he* went inside. I knew that left about three minutes when Pedro would be the only kid still outside. I hid in a tree I knew Pedro would pass under on his way to the door. When I saw him below, I jumped out of the tree onto his shoulders, knocking him to the ground, and then I began to punch him. Obviously, he was stronger than me. But, because of the surprise attack and my anger, I hit him hard and well. I got in some good punches, but finally tough-guy Pedro, bloody and crying, wiggled out from under me and ran inside. I followed, screaming something after him, but I haven't the foggiest idea what. The next thing I remember is three teachers leading me down the hall to the principal's office for what became a two-week suspension, and I saw the nurse tending to the prone body of Pedro right there in the hall."

Josh finished his narrative. "The fact is, Pedro never bothered me again and I got my friends back. But I still feel bad to this day that I lost it, even though I don't know of any other way that I could've dealt with the situation. I guess I feel bad that I didn't just ask my grandparents what to do. That probably would've saved me lots of pain."

"Amazing! That really is an incredible story! Don't worry. I won't beat Eli bloody or anything. I could see why that would be wrong. But the point is that you stood up to him. You made the bully realize that you weren't gonna take any more garbage from him, and he stopped bothering you. So I've got to figure out a way to show Eli that I'm not scared of him anymore and that I'm through with his bullying!"

"I really think that you'd be better off talking to your parents before you do anything," Josh said, rubbing his forehead. Pinny seemed to be ignoring this last point. Josh wondered if he had caused more harm than good.

Pinny began dreaming about the moment that he would best Eli in front of the others. He imagined Eli's face turning all shades of red after he got what he deserved. At the same time, he pushed the various whispers out of his head that were coming from his *yetzer ha-tov*. Those murmurs were reminding him of the prohibition against revenge in the Torah. They passed right through Pinny's consciousness without gaining much notice.

"I'm not sure what I'll do yet," Pinny told Josh, "but it'll be good. See you Friday night!"

CHAPTER FIFTEEN

It wasn't clear who was more nervous that Friday night, *Parshas Vayeishev*. Pinny and Josh were each worried about the planned dinner. Pinny was concerned that maybe Josh would not show up! Also, Pinny was worried that maybe his parents wouldn't approve of Josh by the end of the evening, and they would forbid their friendship to continue.

Josh was even more nervous than Pinny. When he had told him that he knew nothing about Judaism, he wasn't kidding. Zilch. Nada. Zip. Josh wondered what faux pas he would commit in this

Orthodox setting. He was aware that there were many legal restrictions for Orthodox Jews on the Sabbath, and he worried that he might do something that would offend them and embarrass himself. Actually, the only reason he agreed to enter the home of these Orthodox Jews on the Sabbath was what he saw in Pinny. Pinny was mature and exhibited such fine character traits that Josh decided that the Gelbtuchs must be good people too.

Pinny's anxiety was looking like it might have been justified. He had told Josh to come over by about 6:30 pm. By that time, Pinny and his father would have returned from shul and the family would be settled. But Josh had not arrived by 7:00 pm. The Gelbtuchs were like any other large family, and waiting around to start the *seudah* led to bickering and worries of burnt food. Pinny's father, who was reviewing the *parshah* at the dining room table, called out a suggestion. "Perhaps we should begin the meal and Josh will just catch up when he comes," he said.

At that moment, there was a knock on the door. It was Josh, and he was dressed formally. He was wearing a black pinstripe suit with a pleasant sun-yellow tie. Perched precariously on his head was a satin bar-mitzvah yarmulka. Josh had borrowed it from a friend a few hours earlier. He would have been on time, but he had forgotten to buy a gift for his hosts. Not knowing where to get kosher wine, Josh had checked out a few liquor stores before finding one that was open and that carried kosher wine. Josh then bought what he hoped would be acceptable. It was a bottle of concord wine with the name Kedem on its label.

Pinny opened the door and invited Josh inside. "Good Shabbos and thanks for coming!" Pinny gushed as he escorted Josh into the living room. "We were a little worried!"

"Sorry," Josh replied. He'd decided not to explain his tardiness, because it would only underscore his ignorance about Judaism.

Once they'd joined the others, each member of the family wished Josh a warm "Good Shabbos" greeting from their locations scattered around the living room.

"Good Shabbat," Josh answered in reply.

Pinny's father came in from the dining room. Seeing Josh inside, he crossed the room to him with brisk steps and his arms extended. First he clasped Josh's hand inside both of his. Then he pumped Josh's hand enthusiastically and said four or five times, "Good Shabbos, good Shabbos!"

"Please, have a seat. We are just about to sing '*Shalom Aleichem.*' This is a song that we sing to welcome the angels on the Sabbath," Pinny's father explained.

"Tzviki," Mr. Gelbtuch continued, turning to Pinny's eleven year-old brother, "would you bring our guest an English *bentcher*?"

As Tzviki ran to do his job, Pinny led Josh to a spot on the couch. "We'll sit here," he said. At that moment, six-year-old Moishe, who had been eyeing the guest since his appearance and was not adept at dealing with strangers, walked up to the now-seated Josh and stared at his *kippah* for a minute before asking, "Why are you wearing a black teepee on your head?"

Mrs. Gelbtuch raced to Moishe and pulled him toward herself while Moishe protested. "Moishe," she said, "come sit on my lap."

"But I want to know!" Moishe insisted. Some family members like Chedva felt their cheeks becoming red; the whole incident had the potential to make trouble.

Josh came to the rescue. With a serious face he said to Moishe, "Thank you so much for pointing out my mistake! Could you find me a good *kippah* to wear?"

The entire Gelbtuch family let out a sigh of relief. "Yes!" Moishe shouted. "What color do you want? We have black, blue, and green!"

Chapter Fifteen

Mrs. Gelbtuch asked Moishe, "Green? You still have that green yarmulka that I told you to throw in the garbage? It looks like a piece of lettuce!"

Josh said, "I guess I won't do green. How about black?"

As Moishe ran off to get the yarmulka, Tzviki returned with the *bentcher*. Seconds later, Moishe returned with a black velvet yarmulka and helped Josh place it over the curve of his head. Pinny showed Josh the place in the *bentcher* as the family began to sing "*Shalom Aleichem.*"

Mrs. Gelbtuch noticed that it was already 7:30. *Better late than never*, she thought.

Sitting there on the couch, Josh took in the incredible scene. The living room was small, especially when compared with the living room of Josh's youth, which could hold fifty people comfortably. Mr. Gelbtuch sat in a corner in an easy chair that was well-worn and displayed black and blue marks from years of service to an active bunch. He was wearing a dark blue suit with a reddish tie. He was also wearing the felt hat that Josh had seen perched on the heads of other Orthodox Jews. Mr. Gelbtuch's eyes were closed as he rocked gently back and forth to the rhythm of the slow tune he was singing with his rich, melodious voice. In the opposite corner, Mrs. Gelbtuch sat on a love seat with her daughters. The orange two-person couch, now fitting three, clashed strongly with the tan paint on the walls, but somehow seemed just right for this quaint house. Mrs. Gelbtuch was dressed in what could best be described as the royal robe of a queen, while her daughters were dressed like princesses. On the couch next to him on his right, was Pinny, dressed like his father. To his left sat Pinny's four brothers. Each was dressed in a white shirt and black pants. While the singing continued, Josh tried to follow, using the English booklet. Though he wasn't singing, the beautiful sound of the various voices blending together seemed to fill Josh with a feeling of peace. With each passing minute, he felt more comfortable and more relaxed.

When the singing finished, Pinny guided Josh to the dining room. Though it too was small, the space was well-managed. On a shelf in the corner stood two long candlesticks, their flickering flames dancing as their light was reflected by two mirrors mounted on the walls behind the flames. The walls were also decorated with various projects, beginning with some "modern art" drawn right on the actual wall, compliments of a two year old, to the skilled pastel painting, made by a teenage girl, that had been mounted in a wooden frame. The table in the center of the room was bedecked with fine china, silver goblets, and an ornate cloth cover hiding some treasure that Josh wondered about.

"Everyone, please find your seats." Mrs. Gelbtuch's announcement was like the starting gun in a race. Blurs of people racing to find their seats passed Josh. Josh felt Pinny's hand over his and followed the tug. "This is your seat, here next to me," Pinny said.

A brief scuffle broke out among the boys as to who would sit on the other side of the guest. When the dust settled and Mrs. Gelbtuch had stepped in to resolve the disagreement, Moishe was the winner, and he took the other seat next to Josh.

The Shabbos meal began briskly with Kiddush and *hamotzi*. The various courses were, of course, delicious and accompanied by great conversation. Eventually, hours later, all of the children helped clear the dishes. Josh was very impressed with their behavior and, after a dessert of cake and baked apples, when most of them had left the table to play, Josh said as much to Mrs. Gelbtuch.

"You know, I grew up in a very small family, so I don't know what it's like to have lots of kids around. I kind of imagined that everything would be wild and frenzied. Eating a meal would be—again, in my imagination—kind of hit and run, with kids just running around and disinterested in the adult table talk. But your kids…they were here for the meal and they were so involved in the singing and the talk about the Torah portion. And they helped clear the table, to boot! I mean, I am in awe!"

"Thank you so much." The appreciation Mrs. Gelbtuch expressed was sincere. She really welcomed Josh's words of praise. With a smile on her face, she issued a disclaimer. "It's not always like this. We won't invite you over at suppertime on an average school night. It can be a little like feeding time at the zoo!"

Mr. Gelbtuch continued this lighthearted thought, adding, "That's why I try to come home late on a regular basis. I never liked zoos." Seeing mock indignation on his wife's face, he hastily added, "Just kidding! I'm home late because I'm busy with work." Then he winked dramatically as if to say, "I really wasn't kidding!"

Taking advantage of everyone's lighthearted mood, Mrs. Gelbtuch said, "Well, now you see the crazy life Pinny has to contend with daily. Could you please tell us a little about yourself?"

CHAPTER SIXTEEN

Taking a deep breath, Josh began. "Well, I was born in Maryland and grew up in Ocean City. My parents ran a small fast food restaurant called Bill's. They used to serve the classic hot dogs, hamburgers, French fries, and more. Of course they also had fried fish fillet and salads. I remember that we were relatively well-to-do, even for a summer resort city. I don't think the money came from the restaurant. I would guess it came from real estate. We lived in a big house on Fourth Street, which is really close to the water, but my parents owned a few other properties, including an apartment that was above the eatery.

"My parents were both Jewish, but they did not attend any synagogue or anything. Between cooking and their properties, my parents were pretty busy, even during the winter. I remember I went to school by bus in the town of Berlin. The school was Showell Elementary School. We had some really awesome times. Things were going really well. I was an only child, so if there was any noise in the house, I was the one making it."

Here Josh paused. It seemed as if he were attempting to gird himself for what was coming. After a minute, he continued. "Then we had a terrible family tragedy that changed my life forever."

Again, Josh paused. He looked around. All of the children were back in the dining room, either in their seats or on the floor, quietly listening.

"My mother and father…" Josh paused. He was breathing heavily as he thought about the details of the event that he was sharing. "They were on their way home from a conference when a tractor-trailer collided with their car."

The listeners sat spellbound, not moving so as not to break the mood of the moment.

"Thank G-d, neither was killed. It was a miracle. But they no longer were able to care for their greatest treasure—me."

"*Oy vey*, you poor boy." Mrs. Gelbtuch offered Josh a box of tissues to use on his damp eyes, taking one for herself along the way.

Looking around at the serious faces and sad eyes of his audience, Josh tried to lighten the heavy atmosphere that he had created. "I guess I just spoiled the party, huh?"

"What happened next?" Moishe asked eagerly. "This story is exciting! Don't stop now!"

Moishe's innocent comment brought a smile to the adults in the room. Josh even laughed out loud.

"Leave it to a six year old to get the conversation flowing again!" Mr. Gelbtuch commented, chuckling.

"Well, I never thought of my life story in *that* light before. I guess there is a positive spin to everything! I better get on with it so as not disappoint my young friend here."

He continued his autobiography with enthusiasm. "After the life-altering events, I went to live with my father's parents in Baltimore. I continued to be an only child, with a few cousins whom I saw sporadically. At the time, I wasn't very athletic or sociable. Mostly, I developed a strong interest in math and science. I was thoroughly enthralled by everything having to do with the weather.

"I did well in school, although as Pinny knows, I had some social issues. Eventually, my love of science boosted me into the limelight when I created a tool to help scientists know more about the melting glaciers. Eventually, I went to University of Maryland and studied to become a meteorologist. I also learned about climate change. Today, I teach at the university and work on solving the world's climate problems."

Josh ended his account with a big smile. He said, "And of all the good things in my life, nothing was ever as nice as finding a friend named Pinny."

Mr. Gelbtuch had no words. There was no appropriate response that any person in the room could make to such a gushing compliment. Of course, there is a question about whether *teenagers* are people. Pinny's sister, Chedva, had what to say. "Pinny is the nicest thing in your life?" she asked in mock horror. "Man, do you need to get a life!"

For a second, Pinny started to get upset. *How could my sister insult me and my friend like that?* But then he saw a big grin slide across Chedva's face, and Pinny's parents started laughing. Josh too, was laughing. Pinny realized that everyone had taken the comment in the spirit in which it was meant—as a jest! Then, he chuckled as well.

Mr. Gelbtuch announced that since everyone was in the room, they should take the opportunity to *bentch*, so everyone did. Pinny sat next to Josh and helped him read from the English *bentcher*, while Yechiel sat on Josh's lap and tried to read the Hebrew side.

After *bentching*, Josh expressed the need to be on his way, and the whole Gelbtuch family walked him to the door. "It was very nice that you were able to join us this evening. Please come again," Mrs. Gelbtuch encouraged.

"I had a great time. I'll try to come again. Have a great Shabbat." Josh waved as he walked down the steps. "See you again soon. Thanks, Pinny!" With that, Josh reached the sidewalk and swiftly disappeared from view as he turned the corner.

"What a nice man, Pinny," Mrs. Gelbtuch said to her son. "I'm glad we had a chance to meet him. He is such a mentch!"

His mother's compliment made Pinny's heart swell with pride. He had done something right and impressive too!

"Chanale," Pinny's father said to his wife as they left the hallway, "I would like to learn Gemara with Pinny now. Can you and the girls handle the cleanup from the *seudah*?"

"Of course," Pinny's mother answered. "I'd clear the whole table myself if it would help Pinny learn more Torah!" Turning to her daughters, Mrs. Gelbtuch said, "*Nu*, come on girls."

"But, Ma," eleven-year-old Shira protested, "you said you would clear by yourself!"

"When did I ever say anything like that?"

Chedva stepped in to help her sister and herself too. "We heard you say it a second ago…" Her words petered out upon seeing a glare, building in intensity, in her father's eyes. "Oka-ay. We'll do it. Soon."

"Chedva, Shira, go help your mother clear *now*! You know that there's tremendous merit in helping your mother so that Pinny and I can learn. We've had this discussion numerous times and…" Mr. Gelbtuch stopped his shmooze when she saw that the girls had begun to remove the dessert plates.

Instead of rebuke, he said to his girls, "Wow! You are privileged! You are able to earn *Olam haBa* simply by clearing the table. Others work for pennies an hour at this type of job while you are earning a googolplex of reward!" Concluding his words of praise, Mr. Gelbtuch grabbed a *Gemara Bava Metzia* off of the shelf and, together with Pinny, walked down the hallway to the study.

Mrs. Gelbtuch watched her Torah scholars until she saw the door shut. *Nachas* filled her every bone. Chana Gelbtuch knew that she was really lucky to have such a wonderful family.

"Ma, Tatty said we're supposed to *help* clean up, and if you don't join us, then it isn't *helping*." Shira's kvetch made Chana chuckle. *Aren't these kids great? I never know what they're going to do or say. Thank You, Hashem, for all of the gifts You bestow upon me and my family.* With these warm thoughts in mind, Chana headed toward the kitchen. "I'm coming, girls," she called. "I'm coming!"

CHAPTER SEVENTEEN

The American Airlines Arena in Miami, Florida is one of the largest indoor arenas in the United States. It is the home of the Miami Heat, a very old team in the NBA.[16] The original arena was built years ago, but the new, modern facilities had been erected only ten years ago. Modern improvements included built-in media equipment that could be operated remotely. This eliminated visible wires and served

---

16   National Basketball Association.

as an additional revenue source for the facility, as there was fierce competition to have streaming access for the three PMEC, press media equipment centers. Besides the advantage of remote operations, these centers offered incredible court-level viewing and sound. Currently, CNN, NBC, and the local station WTVJ were shelling out millions to make billions.

The digital sign which rose thirty feet into the sky proclaimed "Presidential Debate" in flashing neon colors. The parking lots were full. The streets around the arena had been closed for hours for security reasons. Hordes of venders, selling scorecards and souvenirs, were wandering around and mingling with the Secret Service and state police.

Inside the arena, guards armed with AKL-47s, laser machine guns that were the standard military-issue weapon of choice, stood every dozen yards or so apart. The bustle in the hallways diminished as the debate drew near and ushers guided everyone to their seats. By the starting bell, all of the 19,146 seats were filled with people of all ages and ethnicities. Armed guards stood by the closed door of each exit, while others were scattered throughout the crowd.

The house lights dimmed while the spotlights and stage lights highlighted the stage. It was made of a raised platform on which there were three cloth-covered lecterns. The cloths' colors reflected the parties of each candidate. Red was for the Republican, Vince Pachino. A democratic blue covered Jose Cordova's lectern. Finally, perhaps the most unique color ever displayed in a presidential campaign, was the almond-colored cloth for Independent Carl Almond.

The loudspeaker began with a crackle. Those who had purchased translation headsets put them on, and everyone busied themselves with getting comfortable. The loud noise that filled the full stadium gradually faded into silence.

"Welcome to the last debate between our presidential candidates. This debate is being sponsored by CNN, NBC, AARP,[17] AAA,[18] Boy Scouts of America, and the NRA.[19] Without further delay, let us welcome our moderator for this debate, the newsman's newsman, Mr. Robert Action!"

Deafening clapping filled the stadium as a young, spry, athletically built man, wearing a long-sleeved blue shirt with a bright yellow tie, ran dramatically from behind the crowd, waving to the audience. Reaching the stage, he leaped onto it, avoiding the stairs. "Good evening!" he said into some invisible microphone. The crowd continued clapping.

Robert Action was a man who had put his name to work. By the age of thirty-five, he had already won a Pulitzer Prize and had developed a reputation as a non-biased reporter whose articles were much sought after. He was, without a doubt, the best person to moderate the debate that would most likely decide whom the nation would elect as the next president.

"Good evening," he said again, this time a bit louder. "I am so-o-o happy to be here tonight!" By this time, the audience had quieted down. Action continued speaking, "The greatest aspect of the USA is that the people not only have a say in who should be the president, but they are the only ones who have such a say. In the years past, there was an Electoral College that really determined who became the next president. But with the 38th Amendment, the government is truly elected by the people!"

Loud cheering filled the stadium. The abolishment of the Electoral College had been a big fight and a long time in coming. The original battle took place in the 1960s, resulting in Washington, DC, then not

---

17   American Association of Retired Persons.
18   American Automobile Association.
19   National Rifle Association.

a state, receiving electoral votes with the 23rd Amendment. The next time it was an issue was when the 91st Congress (1969–1971) almost did away with it after Richard Nixon won in the Electoral College, although he had barely had a 1 percent majority in the popular vote.

The most recent fight began after the Electoral College had voted in presidents who had received less than half of the nation's popular vote in four out of the last six presidential contests. The first time was viewed as a fluke. The second time made people angry. The third time that the popular vote had been railroaded, conspiracy theories abounded. Finally, after the fourth time, the new abolitionist movement began. It was precisely this type of situation that worried some of the founding fathers when it was proposed by the Committee of Eleven in 1787. Now, after more than two hundred and fifty years, the people of the United States felt that their vote finally counted.

As the cheering diminished, Action continued his introduction. "Tonight, we welcome the candidates. For the Republicans, let us put our hands together for Vin-n-ce Pa-a-chino!"

Vince Pachino, hands waving above his head in greeting, entered the stage area from behind the curtain and stationed himself by the red-covered podium. Leaning toward the microphone attached to the podium, he shouted in his Chicago accent, "Hello, America!" Pachino was very popular. His stance on many issues reflected the attitude of the lower-income citizens, who represented almost 40 percent of the population. The crowd's cheers turned into a chant. *Vince! Vince! Vince!* The moderator allowed this to continue for a full two minutes before raising his hands and calling for quiet.

"Next," Action announced, "we have the Democratic choice for the highest office in the land. Please welcome Jose-e-e Cordova-a-a!" Cordova came to the stage, pumping his fist in the air. This descendant of Latino parents had a very solid lead in the polls. His ability to speak multiple languages, including Spanish, Portuguese, and Chinese made Jose extremely popular with the minorities. As he passed Vince Pachino, he shook his hand, and Vince thumped his back in response. Cordova then walked to his lectern and greeted the crowd by saying, "*Wanshang hao, buenos noches,* good evening, *Dobry wieczor!*" The multilingual greetings in Chinese, Spanish, English, and even Polish, elicited a rocking response. It took a good five minutes to quiet down the crowd.

Action moved on to the last candidate. "This is such an enthusiastic audience! I'm not sure if the response could be any louder, but let's see how you greet the Independent candidate for president—Carl-l-l Almon-nd!" Almond came onto the stage in a poised and calm way. He displayed an attitude of intensity, as well as one of self-confidence. People sensed his whispered message, "This is a serious job for a serious person who is able to do it. That's me!" Despite his rather subdued entrance, Mr. Almond, governor of Maryland, received applause from a respectable number of people in the audience. Many in the Arena, and perhaps even Robert Action, could not picture Almond as the next president. He seemed too old-fashioned, and he was another white male seeking this high office. But in the free USA, anyone with enough campaign money could run! Leaning in to his microphone, Almond said, "Thank you, Robert, and thank you, people of the USA."

The moderator took charge. "Now that we are all ready to begin, let us review the rules of the debate. I will present a number of questions to each of you, allotting three minutes of response time per candidate. At some point, I will call on some audience members to ask questions of their own. Understood?

"Yes? Well, let's begin. The first question is regarding the Russian Federation. Our love-hate relationship with this foreign superpower is currently in the hate position. We have sanctions against their businesses and have refused exporting quality goods to them—to the detriment of our economy—for their aggressive takeover of parts of the Ukraine for the umpteenth time in the last one hundred years. What would you do to resolve the situation once and for all?"

Republican Vince Pachino replied first. "I think that if we allow Russia to continue in its current ways, we stand to lose a great deal through our financial obligations to help the Ukrainian people and by continuing to expose our soldiers to danger for little gain. Therefore, I would work to shut down the threat in a permanent way. I will not make my plans clear to the public now. But I would aim to end the conflict within six months of taking office."

This approach received a very robust round of applause.

Jose Cordova began his reply with a small chuckle. "I admire my opponent's mafioso approach to the problem." With this allusion to Pachino's Italian roots, Cordova had strategically called attention to a weak spot in the Pachino campaign. There was a question quietly floating around as to whether the Mafia held undue influence over Pachino. Now Cordova had cleverly brought it out in the open, when there was very little time for Pachino's campaign to squelch it before the election.

"I have spoken to many of my Ukrainian *pryyateliv*, friends. As far as they are concerned, they would rather have the fighting end. Let Russia keep their niche of the Ukraine and spare the rest of the region from more bloodshed. So I would work hard to support Ukraine in their bid to grow into a prosperous nation, with an official redrawing of the Russian-Ukrainian border."

A resounding round of applause and cheers issued forth from the crowd. If decibles determined who would become the president, then Cordova had won. The moderator turned to the last candidate.

Carl Almond cleared his throat next to the microphone. "Ah-hem." Quiet reigned. At this point, unintentionally, but to the delight of the crowd, Carl began humming the tune he always hummed when he was giving serious thought to something. *"Hmm, hmm, hm-mm!"* The audience, having heard this tune many times in his commercials, began to hum along. When Carl finished, he was actually surprised to see how many people knew his tune!

Leaning into the mic, Carl said, "If I knew it would become so popular, I would have copyrighted it and collected royalties!"

This surprising joke from the most serious man on the stage created quite a ruckus among the audience. Clapping and cheering, they hummed louder!

Finally, things quieted down and the governor gave his answer. "While I respect the opinions of my fellow candidates, my business background has taught me that nobody takes an important step without giving any thought to the bottom line. Obviously, by easing sanctions and by doing more business with Russia, we can show the Russians that they do not need to swallow other nationals' land to help their bottom line. We could broker an amicable agreement between Russia and the Ukraine that would leave them at peace and appeased.

"That being said, I wish to make it clear here and now that I intend to stock my cabinet with the best experts to advise me. Unlike most presidents, who distribute cabinet positions to their friends or to pay off some political debt, I will hunt for the best consultants, regardless of their party. That has been my policy as governor of the state of Maryland and that will continue to be my strategy. And so, my cabinet members would be the ones who would help me form the country's final response to this situation."

Applause again shook the room as people liked this idea too.

More questions were asked, and each candidate gave strong and consistent replies. Every few questions, when it was Carl Almond's turn to answer, one could hear groups in the audience humming the "Thinking Tune" as he began his answer.

Action knew when it was time to liven things up a little. "Perhaps there is someone out in the audience who wishes to ask a question to these fine gentlemen?" The assemblage seemed to explode. Hands shot up all around the stadium.

CHAPTER EIGHTEEN

Robert Action walked toward the edge of the stage. He peered into the crowd, as if he was searching for a lucky, soon-to-make-the-news person to ask an intelligent question. Finally, his eyes rested on a person in the third row. Action had been planning to call on this man even before he sought audience participation. But, with his skill as a performer after years of public appearances, his act was perfect; nobody could tell that this was a setup.

"Sir," he called out as he pointed, "you in the black hat..." Motioning to one of the ushers, Robert said, "Bring that man a microphone, please." The usher handed the mic to the black-hatted man as Robert concluded what he was saying, "Do you have any questions for the candidates?"

The fellow in the black hat stood up. "I think I *do* have a question," he said. The moment that he began to speak, the crowd went into a frenzy! It was George Wong, the current president!

Robert Action signaled to someone who was standing in one of the media booths, and "Hail to the Chief," the Presidential Anthem of the United States, began to play over the loudspeaker. Action called out over the music, "Mr. President! Come on up here and say hello!"

Obligingly, the president, followed by his security detail, who were all wearing black suits and earpieces, made his way to the stage. One by one, the president shook hands with Action and the three candidates.

Whoever had come up with this plan (probably it was Robert Action, but he wasn't saying) was brilliant. The cheering showed just how much the crowd appreciated the surprise. People liked the idea of challenging the presidential hopefuls with real White House issues.

"Mr. President," the moderator's words over the loudspeaker brought quiet to the massive room, "please, ask away."

"Thank you, I will. As president, I have been criticized time and again for sustaining social programs by raising taxes. Some middle-class people now pay 40 percent in income tax. How would you keep the welfare programs going without increasing taxes?"

The president asked a few more tough questions and then took his leave to a standing ovation. Had it not been for the term limits on the office of the president, George Wong would have been reelected. The first president of Asian descent, George brought honesty, integrity, and humanity to a position that had become home to elitist, corrupt, and sometimes incompetent people.

The evening's debate was coming to a close. All of the candidates were emitting signs of weariness. Action looked at his notes. Then, lifting his head, he smiled and spoke into his microphone.

"Friends, I have been saving the best question for last. At this moment of waning strength, I will ignite the passion and fire by asking: Given the melting of the polar caps and the rapidly rising ocean levels and the increasing average temperatures—currently almost 10°F more than fifty years ago worldwide—many countries are racing to protect themselves from the effects of global warming. What would you, as president of the most powerful nation in the world, suggest that we do—say for Florida, which is more than 20 percent under water already, and for the rest of the world—to ensure the survival of mankind?"

The spectators loved this frosting on the debate's cake. Pachino hemmed and hawed and tried to explain that the weather went through cycles, and although things looked bad now, the future was going to be brighter.

He was relieved when Action turned the question over to Cordova. But he fared no better. He was able to sound more convincing, but ultimately, he talked circles around the issue without offering any concrete answer.

Almond was unruffled by the question. He delivered his answer with poise and confidence. "As I mentioned earlier, I intend to staff my cabinet with experts. This includes scientists for all kinds of issues. As many of you know, I am the only governor in the country with a meteorologist on staff. He has helped us through many storms, and most prominently, Atlantis. So I do not have a specific answer now, however, I have a plan for addressing the issue immediately upon becoming your next president."

An eruption of applause shook the room. Carl Almond displayed a competency and no-nonsense approach to problem solving that was rare in politics.

Governor Almond's comments carried even greater weight, since his was the last response of the evening. Robert Action wrapped things up, expressing gratitude to the president, candidates, sponsors, support staff, audience, and various others, and ended with the cliché, "May the best man win!"

CHAPTER NINETEEN

The sun was shining, trying mightily to pierce the bubble of Arctic weather that had brought the mercury to -5°F on this crisp February morning. Pieces of frost, each as if placed by an artist with meticulous care and reason, decorated Josh's bedroom window with a silvery sheen, refracting the sunlight into a rainbow of colors. Most people were waking up in cold bedrooms, as the drop in temperature had been dramatic overnight. Josh, with the advanced warning of weather conditions that all meteorologists enjoy, had set his home thermostat to crank up the heat an hour before he had to get out of bed. Josh also had the luck of living in a newly upgraded apartment. This meant that the floors were heated, so stepping on the shiny hardwood floors was actually pleasurable on wintry mornings.

However, for the moment, none of this mattered to Josh. He was still buried under his down quilt in a heavy slumber. He was dreaming. He was a lecturer in the United Nations, urging them to halt their plans to solve global warming. It was not clear what their plans were, but his speech was powerful. A vote was called to see if the nations of the world would heed his request. One by one,, the nations cast their votes. His dream was so real that Josh was sweating from nervous anticipation of the pending results!

The shrill *beep, beep, beep* of his alarm clock yanked Josh from his pseudo-reality, depriving him of finding out how the vote went. It was 9:00 am, and time for Josh to get up. Turning over, Josh hit the snooze button; he disagreed with the dictate of his electric nemesis. He could sleep for a little longer; after all, it was his day off. Seven minutes later, Josh was again roused by beeping. This time he groped for the clock and shut it for good. But half a second later, there was ringing again! Josh sat up and looked for its source.

The offender was on the counter in his kitchen, a few feet from his bed in the small studio apartment. The phone was ringing. Josh climbed out of bed to answer the call and tripped every few steps over his blanket which was wrapped around his legs.

"Uh...hello? Good morning, Josh here," he said into the phone.

"Josh? It's Harold. Harold Silver from the university. Sorry to bother you, but I need a favor."

Josh rubbed his tired eyes. He knew what was coming. Ever since he had commented to some fellows in the faculty lounge that he was interested in extra teaching opportunities to earn some extra cash, he was called once or twice a week to fill in for a professor who could not make it to his lesson. Sometimes he did it. But when he was asked to lecture about ancient Egyptian civilization or basket weaving (really, there is such a course!), Josh refused. It was Harold's job to find substitute professors to fill these spots.

"All right, Harold, what do you want me to teach about this time? The cultural impact of Star Trek?" Josh asked as he put the phone on speaker so he could dress.

"I have a topic I know you will love! It is actually a special alumni lecture for the visiting Class of '40. You know they came for 'A Weekend of Memories'? Well, Professor Kulo, who actually taught many in the group, was supposed to lecture them on global warming, but he had a heart attack last night! So we were going to cancel the lecture, but when the university bigwigs heard about it, they called me. It seems that this topic is near and dear to two of those alumni. Their names are Sam and Kara Woodrop. Do you know who they are?"

Josh did not, and he said so.

"They're the owners of Natural Electrics, the big, environmentally-safe energy source company that is valued at a cool five *billion* dollars! They are extremely devoted to dealing with global warming. Besides the dollar signs that they represent to the university, they are very well-connected politically. As we speak, the Woodrops and the other alums are having breakfast with President Almond! He is seen as a leader in addressing general environmental issues, and his company, AAP, is known to be one of the top-rated companies by Save the Planet. Well, the entire board of directors called me to tell me that if I don't make sure that the lecture goes on, then I would be out of a job!

"I asked them, 'What do you want me to do—pretend to be the professor who just had the heart attack? Or maybe we can get him to lecture from his hospital bed.' They said, 'Do whatever it takes.'

"I was stuck. I spoke to the dean and she said that if we find an expert in environmental issues, we'll be okay. So guess who I thought of?"

Josh laughed. "Okay, Harold, you got me. I would love to talk about good old global warming. Tell me what I need to know: time, place, etc."

"Josh, you are the best. Thanks so much! I'll recommend that the university double your salary! Though my input might not get you very far. So, after breakfast with the president, the group is going to play a little golf, of course. After lunch, they'll gather in the main lecture hall for your talk. Probably around 2:00 pm. That gives you plenty of time to prepare, doesn't it?"

"Harold, thanks for your vote of confidence. Can I give them homework? Like bring me $1 million in cash by tomorrow so my private work can continue?"

"Sure, Josh, but their next reunion isn't for a couple of years!" Harold wished Josh the best and told him to call if he needed anything for the lecture. He provided Josh with his private cell phone number and then added, "But only call if it's an emergency!" Harold then hung up.

Josh felt energized. This was fun for him! With newfound energy, he finished dressing and began to prepare his talk. Although Josh would not admit it to himself, lurking in the back of his mind was the hope that this talk would turn out to be more than a simple chance to share his expertise. He was hoping it would also fill the coffers of his research and development for climate stability.

By 1:45 pm, Josh was in the hall and ready to talk. He was nervous, which was a good sign. He had double- and triple-checked that the audio/visual system was working properly. He had made sure that his watch, which also served as his cell phone and his portable computer, was charged and fully operational.

He had dressed for the part. Wearing a gray suit and blue tie covered with oceanic images, Josh presented a refreshing, natural look of a climate expert. As he waited, he adjusted his tie, refolded his handkerchief, and shuffled his notes. Harold called to "touch base," which could be interpreted to mean that he was checking that Josh was there.

Five minutes before the lecture was to begin, Josh placed himself by the entrance of the room, checking his reflection in the door's glass and brushing down some stubborn hairs with his hand. The guests arrived at 2:00 pm. As they entered, Josh wished them a good day. Not knowing that Josh was the newly scheduled expert who would be giving the talk, most thought that he was simply a guide provided by the university.

"Hey there, fellow," one of the guests called to Josh, "could you direct me to the restrooms?"

Josh sent the man in the proper direction.

"Kara, let's ask this gentleman." Josh turned to see a tall couple, dressed informally. "Sir, would you carry this suitcase down to the front for us?" The inquirer was wearing a name tag that said Sam Woodrop. "It contains some materials pertaining to global warming, as well as mementos of our weekend here at the university," Sam explained.

Josh silently carried the suitcase to the front of the room and found a folding table set up by one of the maintenance people. Sam and Kara watched as Josh placed the suitcase on the table and stood there as if waiting for something. In his mind, Josh rolled his eyes and thought, *Rich people!* Then he realized that they were waiting for him to open the suitcase and set up the display. So that's what he did.

The Woodrops retreated to where the rest of the alumni were sitting and impatiently waiting for the speaker to enter. Josh headed to the front of the room.

On his way, he overheard one alumnus say to another, "Things haven't changed a bit! We used to wait so long for the professors! In my business, if you come late more than three times, you're fired! That's the attitude I'd take if I were in charge!" Josh recognized the speaker's voice as the man who had asked for directions to the restrooms. Sighing at the holier-than-thou attitude of some people, Josh turned on his lapel microphone and said, "Welcome to my talk on global warming."

His unexpected start had people scrambling for seats. From where Josh stood, it looked like a game of musical chairs for adults.

When everyone was settled and finished whispering about how the speaker was way too young to be an expert about the climate, Josh began. "My name is Dr. Josh Green. I am a meteorologist and a climatologist. I am known for inventing the PRIME scope. I am currently on staff at the university, teaching about meteorology, and I have a private venture business to develop a sustainable plan for climate stability."

Having swiftly established his credentials, Josh looked around the room and saw some faces that were blushing with embarrassment for suspecting that Josh was unqualified. Others were glowing with excitement. They looked forward to what Josh would say.

"The history of active discussion about climate change began in 1859. John Tyndall, a physicist with the Royal Institute of Great Britain, discovered that some gases blocked infrared radiation. This led to a theory that gases trapped in the atmosphere could lead to climate change.

"The discussion took a turn to define this climate change as a warming of the globe when, in 1896, Nobel Prize winner Svante Arrhenius proved that increases in carbon dioxide in the atmosphere lead to global warming. The theory seemed to gain legitimacy when Guy Stewart Callendar discovered the Callendar Effect and charted an increase in global temperatures of almost one degree over just forty years. This took place in 1938. Callendar viewed this change as good, since it would keep shipping routes through the Arctic clear of ice.

"In 1945, the US government began to invest in studies on climate change, with an official meeting about the effects of such changes taking place in Colorado in 1965. In 2006, the evidence of global warming was considered conclusive. The earth was changing, and not at a slow pace.[20] Since then, there has been ongoing debate as to the causes, extent, and effects of global warming.

"Ultimately, a large part of the debate revolves around the cause. Is it human-initiated, as some say, or is there another cause? One theory is that it is connected to the sun—that the variations in solar flaring and sunspots are consistent with the increased global temperatures.

"Today we have more certain knowledge. We know for a fact that in 1910, President Taft signed a bill establishing an area in Montana as Glacier National Park. Then, it had 150 glaciers. Today, it has none. Also, the Himalayan glaciers are totally gone.

"The freshwater ice breakup in the Northern Hemisphere now occurs twenty days earlier and freezes twenty-two days later than it did in the late 1800s. Melting Arctic ice has increased ocean levels by more than one-and-a-quarter feet. Metropolises like Tokyo, Shanghai, New York, and others, are in grave danger. Countries like Tuvalu, a small country in the South Pacific, have disappeared despite their attempts to plan for the rising waters.

"Also, erosion is a matter of great concern. Freshwater pollution is something that has been addressed through desalination at a cost of increased energy usage, which may further the warming effect."[21,22]

Josh continued to discuss the issues of global warming for a full hour. He showed slides of the Arctic ice before the year 2000 and in current times. He showed charts and graphs that traced the earth's

---

20   http://www.aip.org/history/climate/timeline.htm.
21   http://environment.nationalgeographic.com/environment/global-warming/big-thaw.
22   http://www.scientificamerican.com/article/why-dont-we-get-our-drinking-water-from-the-ocean.

temperature, solar flares, carbon gas increases, and pictures of tree ring studies.

His audience was drinking up every word he said. They were absorbing his intense and information-packed presentation like sponges absorbing water. Each person felt that this hour was the best of the entire weekend.

Josh concluded his talk with, "We must find a way to protect the planet. Only with a protected planet will we prevent the mass extinction of the most important mammals—humans. Thanks for listening."

The applause was deafening. It continued for almost two full minutes.

Sam and Kara hurried to the front of the lecture hall and extended their hands, thanking him and apologizing for asking such an educated man to set up their materials. Josh demurred. "No need to apologize. After all, I'm a person. I can help someone, even though I know about climate change."

"We know, but…" Sam thought to argue with Josh's humility, but changed his mind. "Young man, do you have a business card? I think I may want to contact you in the future for other talks."

Josh reached into his pocket and took out one of his university faculty business cards. "I'm honored that you enjoyed my words so much," he said. Remembering that he had one card from his climate venture in his wallet, he added, "One second. Let me give you another card that I have for my private work on climate issues." Josh handed Sam the card.

As Sam and Kara began to walk away, Kara called out, "Thanks again. We were really inspired! You are a very impressive young man. I see you holding positions of importance in the future! Good luck."

Other alumni came by and shared similar sentiments. They related how inspired and impressed they were. Each wished him good luck, and a couple gave Josh their business cards, "in case you are ever in our neighborhood."

After conversing with Josh, many alumni stopped by the Woodrops' table of goodies to collect some of the pamphlets and logo-emblazoned promotional items that the Woodrops had provided. Josh made his way to the table and picked up a T-shirt with the words "Global warming is in *your* hands" written across the front. He also grabbed a couple of mugs with the university crest and the year '35 stamped below. He had no use for the pamphlets. Any useful information on the climate was in his head or his computer. As for the other Save the Planet stuff, Josh simply didn't have much interest.

Josh returned to the front of the room and collected his belongings. He double-checked to make sure that he had not left anything behind and then exited the hall. As he was leaving, Josh's phone rang.

"Hello?"

"Josh, my buddy, it's Harold. I gotta hand it to you. You rate big time! Just five minutes ago, the chairman of the board of the university called me. He thanked me for getting 'the expert' to fill in. He said he hates to say it, but he's glad the other professor had to cancel, because 'the expert's speech'—that's your speech—was very lucrative for the university's endowment fund. He told me that the Woodrops dropped a check for six figures on his desk, with a pledge for another in a month or two! Now the chairman is so happy with me that he gave me a raise!"

Josh asked the obvious question. "And, Harold, what about me? Will I see a raise? Will the chairman express his pleasure with my performance?"

Suddenly Harold seemed to develop phone trouble. "What? Josh? You're breaking up. Call me later." With this, there was the discernable click of the phone connection being terminated.

Just my luck, Josh thought. *I help him out and he forgets to give credit where credit is due. I bet he didn't even tell the chairman that I'm the one who gave the talk. He probably just said that he got an expert, and the chairman didn't care who it was as long as it generated a lot of donations!*

Shaking his head in disappointment, Josh headed home. To help himself feel better, Josh thought about the fact that he would receive payment for the talk, just like he had been remunerated for similar talks in the past. It was not really fair to expect anything more than that. This was how life was in the big leagues.

Had Josh known what would come out of his talk, disappointment would have been the last thing on his mind.

CHAPTER TWENTY

The bell had already summoned the boys into their classrooms, but Pinny remained by his locker. In his hands, he held a thick envelope. The envelope was bulging with cash. He had all of the school trip money he had raised tucked inside. There was $250 from his very profitable chocolate candy sales and $150 from his raffle ticket sales. The total $400 was a lot to keep in his backpack. At least that is what his mother had told him before he left for school that morning.

Pinny recalled their brief discussion. "Pinny, please let me write a check for all of that cash!" his mother had begged.

"Ma, I'm bar mitzvah! I'm responsible! I won't lose it. Don't you trust me?"

His mother tried to convince him that it was *more* responsible to bring a check to school. But Pinny had insisted. Having such a large sum of cash would impress his friends, and Pinny planned to do just that. This would squelch the rumor that someone, maybe Eli or his friends, had started: that Pinny was too poor to be able to pay for the trip. Well, Pinny would prove them wrong!

Once a week, at the end of the day, all of the eighth-grade boys would gather in the lunchroom for a meeting about their class trip. There, Rabbi Fried, the *rebbi* in charge of fundraising, would collect trip money from those who had brought, as well as discuss possible fundraising ideas and review the intinerary for the trip. Pinny planned that there, in front of all of the boys—many of whom had not yet brought in their money—Pinny would walk up to Rabbi Fried and slowly, in a loud voice, count out the $400. Pinny would then proclaim that this was just to pay for the school trip, and that he had raised an additional $50 for spending money that he still had at home. He hoped that the person guilty of spreading the rumor about him would squirm with embarrassment and realize that *lashon ha-ra* sometimes comes back to bite the speaker!

Carefully placing the envelope in one of the pockets inside his backpack, Pinny then stowed it in his locker and headed to his science class. Since he had waited for the hall to clear of students before checking his money, he was now ten minutes late.

Pinny made his way to his classroom and gently opened the classroom door. He tried stealthily sneaking to his seat in the back of the room. He had already been late twice this quarter, and a third lateness would result in a detention after school.

The teacher was facing the board and writing something, and the class was full of low-volume chatter. Eli Truxenberg watched as Pinny almost reached his seat with his tardiness unnoticed.

"Pinny," Eli said loudly in feigned concern, "is everything all right? Class started ten minutes ago." The teacher turned around quickly. Pinny prepared for the worst. To his surprise, the woman in the front of the class was not Mrs. Bondroff, the regular science teacher! It was a substitute. Pinny whispered a small *tefillah* of thanks to Hashem.

"Young man? You are late! Please get a late note."

Pinny stuttered for a moment before he started babbling. "Ah...b-bu-ut...uh...please, I'm so sorry I'm late. I had a really urgent thing I had to do..."

The substitute didn't really care, so she said, "Fine. But I will report it to Mrs. Bondroff in my notes on the day. What's your name?"

A mischievous gleam came into Pinny's eyes. He realized that here was an opportunity to stand up to Eli's abuse, even though it entailed a small lie. Glancing in Eli's direction, Pinny was glad to see that Eli was busy conversing with one of his henchmen. Pinny walked up to the teacher's desk. "My name is Eli Truxenberg," he said quietly. The teacher leaned onto the desk and wrote that name in her notes.

Pinny had almost pulled it off. He would have succeeded in his prank had it not been for his mother. As Pinny turned to go back to his seat with a satisfied feeling of revenge in his heart, an annoying voice wafted through the loudspeaker. "Pinny Gelbtuch, please come to the office immediately."

Half of the class pointed at Pinny and said, "Oooh! Pinny's in trou-ble!" The confused substitute teacher looked from Pinny to the pointing students and began to speak. Pinny, not wishing to face her wrath, simply walked out of the room without comment. It was only later that Pinny found out that the substitute had spent the next five minutes sorting out the mess, enabling Eli to learn of the deception Pinny had attempted.

For now, though, Pinny headed to the office. He could not imagine the purpose of the summons. His grades were fine and his behavior was generally good. What could be wrong?

"Pinny Gelbtuch here," he announced to Mrs. Gold, the secretary, as he leaned into the little window that put some distance between her and whoever wanted to speak to her.

"Pinny, your mother just called and told me that you have a large sum of cash for the class trip in your backpack and she is nervous about it. She asked me to hold it until Rabbi Fried comes and then give it to him directly."

Lots of unpleasant thoughts skittered across Pinny's mind as he thought of his mother at this moment. Pinny wasn't *chutzpadik*, but in one fell swoop, he thought, *She doesn't trust me. She went behind my back. She ruined my chance to get back at Eli. She got me in trouble with the teacher.* That kind of damage would make most people a little *chutzpadik*. "Mothers," he muttered darkly under his breath.

Pinny slowly made his way to his locker, fished the envelope out of his backpack, and even more slowly, trudged back to the office with the money. Mrs. Gold flashed him a big smile as she took it. "Wow! There's a lot in here! Did you raise all of this yourself?" Pinny confirmed that he had.

"Impressive! Well, here's a note for class. See you later."

The praise felt good. Pinny tried really hard to hold on to his frustration and anger so that he could accurately express himself later, when he would tell his mother how hurt he felt because of her mistrust. But Mrs. Gold had meant it when she said that she was impressed, and that made Pinny feel happier.

Despite feeling a little better, he still did not want to go back to class. The note would cover the time he was gone, but he had no way to repair the damage caused by his lateness and his lie. Pinny spent the next twenty minutes alternating between the water fountain, his locker, and the bathroom. Next period was gym, so five minutes before the bell rang, he headed in that direction.

CHAPTER TWENTY-ONE

"What are we playing today, Coach?" Pinny asked Coach Simmons when he got to the school's gymnasium.

"Hockey. Inside. If you want to help, you can take out the equipment for me," the coach answered as he retied a shoelace.

When his class entered the gym, Pinny seamlessly fell in with them. A few boys tried to ask him about his office visit, but Pinny made it clear that he was not going to discuss it. As the captains began to pick their teams, Nesanel came over to him. Thinking that Nesanel wanted to know why he'd been called out of class, Pinny started to walk away from him.

"Pinny," Nesanel called as he took a quick step and grabbed Pinny's arm, "I'm not going to ask you anything. I'm here to warn you. Eli knows about your attempt to get him in trouble, and he's planning to get back at you for it. I'd be worried about that during a game like hockey."

"What should I do?" Pinny asked, frightened. "I can't tell the coach anything without getting myself in trouble!"

Nesanel was honest. "I don't know. But at least now you know about it."

"Thanks, Nesanel," Pinny answered sincerely. "Thanks for your warning."

The game began with typical middle-school boy competitiveness. The boys used their sticks, feet, and bodies to get the puck into the others team's goal. The coach blew his whistle so much that it was hard to figure out when one tweet was ending and the next one beginning.

Pinny and Eli were on different teams, but since Pinny played right wing and Eli center, they spent the first half of the game at opposite ends of the field. Coach Simmons was pretty strict that their games be played by the real rules, so generally, offensive players did not end up on their goalie's side of the court.

After a short break for drinks, the boys began the second half of the game. This time, Pinny's captain switched things around and Pinny played as a defenseman. Eli remained in his position at center. For most of the half, things seemed in order. True, Eli made gross and mean faces whenever he passed by Pinny, but Pinny stepped out of his way whenever Eli made a drive, allowing his fellow defensemen to pick up the slack.

The game was tied at 3–3. Eli had the puck and was heading toward the goal. Only a minute or two remained for the game.

Pinny glanced to see one of the other defenseman fall over an opposing player's stick that may or may not have been placed there on purpose to cause the fall. It didn't matter. What mattered was that Eli was barreling toward the goalie and it was Pinny's job to stop him.

The students who had gym next period had already come in, and, like many others, did not like Eli and did not want to see him score. They began to chant, "Pinny!" (*clap clap*) "Pinny!" (*clap clap*) "Pinny!" (*clap clap*). They were urging Pinny to go all out for defense! Not having much of a choice, Pinny hurried and placed himself squarely in Eli's path.

◆

Eli claimed that he couldn't stop. He cited his clear attempt to turn away before impact as proof that the incident was out of his control. Pinny's teammates argued and said that Eli did it because he wanted to get back at Pinny. Whichever it was, the result was the same. Eli's left shoulder smashed into Pinny's right upper arm. The crunch of broken bone sounded like a gunshot. Pinny's agonizing screams sounded like those of a gunshot victim.

Pinny fell to the floor, writhing in pain. Coach Simmons hustled over to the huddle of boys gathering around their fallen comrade. "Nesanel, call Rabbi Finegold," he ordered.

The coach took one look at Pinny's arm, saw red and jagged ivory protruding from where it did not belong, and almost passed out. Then his adrenaline kicked in. Coach Simmons blew his whistle and yelled, "By the time I count to ten, I want this place cleared out! One. Two. Three…"

Everyone hurried to leave. Though they were curious and concerned, the sight of the usually calm Coach Simmons getting upset motivated them to listen. Heading to their classes or standing just outside the gym, the students argued and debated the event. Accident? Intentional? Broken? Dead? Every possibility was discussed.

After the initial impact, Eli was stunned. Though not hurt, the wind had been knocked out of him since Pinny had been stationary. Now, as the place cleared out, Eli got up to leave. "Where are you going, young man?" Coach thundered. "You hurt him real bad. Now you're going to see just how much damage you caused!"

Eli sat down on the floor. He was worried that he would get into serious trouble. Someone might tell Coach about what had happened earlier that day and he'd figure out that Eli had slammed into Pinny on purpose. *Well, nobody can prove that I did it on purpose,* Eli thought. *As long as I act the right way, no one will know.*

He got up and made his way over to where the coach and Pinny were. "Pinny, I am so sorry. I just couldn't stop." Eli forced his eyes to tear up. "Please forgive me!"

Pinny just groaned. The pain was so intense that he felt himself losing consciousness. Coach Simmons kept talking, "Pinny, hang in there. Help is on the way. Talk to me. I know you're in terrible pain. Squeeze my finger with your left hand. That's good."

By this time, the *menahel* and school nurse had come into the gym. After a brief glance, the nurse took Rabbi Finegold aside. "Rabbi, obviously he has a serious complex fracture. I am sure he'll need surgery to repair the damage, plus he's bleeding a lot. We should get him to a hospital quickly."

Rabbi Finegold took out his cell phone and called Mrs. Gold. "Mrs. Gold? Please call the Gelbtuchs and tell them that Pinny got hurt during gym. We are calling an ambulance to take him to the hospital emergency room. Give them my cell number and tell them that as soon as I can, I will call them. Also, send a student over to me with Pinny's insurance information and emergency forms." Finishing with these practical instructions, Rabbi Finegold dialed 911.

Six minutes later, the EMT[23] crew arrived. With the dexterity and efficiency of practiced professionals, they carefully transferred Pinny from the floor of the gym to a stretcher. Then they carried him out of the building to the accompaniment of wishes for a *refuah sheleimah* from the many concerned students who had been waiting around in the halls for some news about Pinny's condition. The EMTs loaded Pinny into the back of the ambulance and one medic got in with him. The other medic then headed to the driver's seat, and Rabbi Finegold climbed into the front passenger seat and they sped away.

---

23 Emergency Medical Technicians.

CHAPTER TWENTY-TWO

President Almond sat at the Resolute desk in the oval office, eating some jelly beans. His first few months as commander in chief had been pretty tranquil. There had been no US-involved wars, no budget crisis, and the general attitude of the public was positive. Talk show hosts were very busy with state issues or the Supreme Court, which had a number of high-profile cases. They were not criticizing the "new kid on the block."

There *was* food for their discussions. Almond had been putting together his cabinet and replacing various ambassadors in order to have his "Shield of Educated Experts," called "SEE" for short. The nickname was coined by a reporter some time during the elections, and it stuck. Actually, it was the reason Almond won the election. Voters saw the quality and the value of the SEE that he had set up as governor of Maryland and realized its great potential on the national level.

As with every political position, each person that President Almond selected for the cabinet was loved by some and hated by others. In the past, most presidents had to defend their choices for the members of the inner circle, but oddly enough, there was almost no opposition to any of Almond's choices. Even those with some objections seemed to appreciate the overall package that made up the president's cabinet and kept quiet.

That's why the three major snowstorms that hit the East Coast and the ice storms in the Midwest received special presidential attention. Though the cities' immobilizing ice and eight feet of accumulated snow did not warrant a national state of emergency or Disaster Area declaration, President Almond had his expert meteorologist, Mark Malone, keep him well-informed about the severe weather, and he arranged for Mark to appear nationally to offer "expert" input about the weather.

The president himself made visits to the affected areas, staying in local hotels, eating in the working man's eateries, and creating havoc for the Secret Service, who had to figure out the logistics of protecting the president in all of these locations. The people loved it! The president's approval rating rose to nearly 90 percent, and for the first time in decades, the American nation was feeling hopeful.

Looking around the Oval Office with a feeling of pride, Almond's eyes came to rest on the Seal of the President—bearing a red, white, and blue shield guarding an eagle clutching thirteen arrows of war in one talon and a thirteen-leaf olive branch representing peace in the other—woven into the beige and brown carpet. His eyes then shifted past the pair of sofas and assorted tables and chairs in the center of the rug and focused on the paintings that had been hanging on the walls since Franklin D. Roosevelt decorated the then newly built room in 1934. Directly opposite where he was sitting was a portrait of the first president, George Washington, beneath which was the neoclassical white marble mantel that was in the original Oval Office, built in 1909. On the wall to his left was a painting of President Abraham Lincoln, opposite the tall grandfather clock built by John Seymour of Boston in the late 1700s. The president had chosen to keep the decorations to a minimum. Everything that he selected to have in the room was a piece of history and served as a testament to the durability of democracy.

Almond rubbed his hands together in anticipation of his afternoon briefing with his chief of staff, Allen Parker. Keeping Parker as part of the team underscored Carl's goal of efficiency through relying on experts. Allen was the best. He knew how to manage the president's schedule in order to get the most out of each day. He was also well-liked and respected by politicians of every party. Parker was good at getting things done exactly how President Almond wanted and expected them to be done.

Chief of Staff Parker came in swiftly, setting down a sheaf of papers on the coffee table between the couches. Sitting down on one of them, he let out a deep sigh. "So, my dear friend, you ready for today's challenges?"

"Don't be so dramatic, Allen. What's the issue?"

"Well, did you know that the GCGW is coming up?"

President Almond had learned long ago that if something had an acronym, *then* and only then, was it important. "What in the world is that? If I were playing Balderdash, I'd say it stands for Green Cat Grappling Wrestlers! By the way, I really enjoyed playing that game with those school kids last week!"

Parker rolled his eyes. "Well, if you want, we could arrange a weekly game here at the White House. Instead of your continuing to guess, I will tell you. Global Conference on Global Warming, or GCGW for short, is, to quote their website, 'a multidisciplinary international conference on global warming and climate change issues and potential solutions, aiming to provide a forum for the: exchange of technical information, dissemination of high-quality research results, presentation of new policy and scientific developments, and promotion of future directions and priorities for more sustainable energy in the future.' Whew!" Parker ended his sentence with a dramatic blast of exhaled air.

"Wow! That is powerful!" Almond straightened his tie. "Could you say that again?"

The chief of staff rolled his eyes again. Almond had developed a weird sense of humor since he had taken office. Often at Parker's expense.

The president smiled. "Relax, my friend. I was teasing. Seriously though, from the way you began telling me about this conference, I discern an urgency. What could be urgent about a topic that is so talked about and so difficult to do much about?"

"Well, sir," Parker often addressed the president more formally when he was anxious or upset. The president's casual attitude about climate change bothered him. Climate change was a fact. To save the planet would take action. The president's casual attitude suggested inaction.

Parker continued, "We need to send someone there to represent the US. Following your policy, we need an expert. This meeting takes place in Athens in a couple of months and our expert needs to be there. But there is actually an additional urgency. We have learned of a scheduled closed-door meeting between a number of representatives of nations that have radical plans to protect themselves from the effects of the rising seas and loss of land and the other damage caused by the continuation of global warming. If we are going to have a say in what is wise and safe for the world to do, we need to develop a viable approach!"

Carl adopted a more serious attitude. He really did recognize the importance of the global warming discussion and, as a person who set standards in other areas of environmental protection, he did not take the planet's future lightly. He was just baiting his chief. "Okay, so the question is how do we find such an expert?"

Humming his "Thinking Tune," President Almond paced back and forth on the shiny hardwood floor that framed the rug. "*Hmm, hmm, hm-mm.*" Then he snapped his fingers at the same time Parker did. "Mark Malone," they said to each other in unison. Saying the unnecessary, Carl continued, "Our expert meteorologist probably knows of experts on the climate!"

Pressing the button on his intercom, the president asked his secretary to get a message to Mr. Malone that the president wanted to meet with him as soon as possible. As they waited to see if Mark would respond right away, the president and his chief of staff continued discussing the other items on the day's agenda.

"You're meeting with Senator Jacobson and his committee today at 2:00 pm to discuss the tax idea that he is proposing. All of the statistics that you requested are in the two binders your secretary will bring you in a little bit. The secretary of state would like to discuss with you the whole East Africa situation before he heads out. I would think that you would just let the warring factions fight it out..."

The president lifted his hand, cutting Parker off and indicating that he wanted to speak. "Is Sadiki Azikiwe coming to the meeting also?" Sadiki Azikiwe was an immigrant from East Africa who was an expert on the people and politics of that part of the world.

"Yes, and a few others. But again, sir, if you don't mind my saying so..."

Again the president stopped Parker mid-sentence. "Okay, I get it. Let's discuss things when the whole group is here. What else is on my plate? Anything fun?"

"Tomorrow evening you're having dinner with Sam and Kara Woodrop here in the Family Dining Room. They've invited a number of friends to join them, and they have all been cleared by security."

Buzz, buzz, buzz. The noise indicated that the president's secretary was calling him on the intercom. Almond answered it, "Yes?" Chirping emitted from the other end. It sounded like an angry bird. "I understand. I will certainly... Of course! No. You're right... uhh...but...okay. Anything else? That's perfect! We're waiting. Thank you!"

Turning to his chief of staff, the president sighed, then smiled and said, "She informed me that one of my children slid down the banister that leads to the State Floor just as a tour group was on its way up the steps! I got a speech about the dignity of the presidential family and a report on the tour guide who was accidentally kicked. I'm supposed to punish the offender later today."

Though the president did not name the offender, only one of the president's four children seemed the likely culprit. Twelve-year-old Carl Jr., the youngest, was always causing a ruckus somewhere. What was funny was the president's pledge to discipline. Carl Sr. treasured his little one and spoiled him! Mr. Parker thought about whether *this* time warranted some friendly parenting advice, but decided against it.

"Oh," the president suddenly remembered, "she also told me that Mark Malone said he was coming right away."

As if on cue, there was a knock on the door. Parker stood up and answered it. Malone was there, holding an umbrella in his left hand. Both the president and his chief were perplexed. The sun was shining and the weather report, given to them in person by the man in the doorway, was for a clear day! Noticing the puzzled looks on their faces, it took a moment for Malone to understand and remark, "Don't worry! I left it in the Press Briefing Room last week and just remembered to go get it today." Even with the months that had passed since their first meeting, Malone was still not totally comfortable around Carl Almond.

"No problem. I didn't mean to make you feel uncomfortable. Please, come in. Have a seat. Allen and I were having a discussion and wondered if you could help us solve a problem we're facing."

Mark came into the room and sat at the end of one of the couches. He did not lean back; rather, he sat perched on the edge of the seat as if ready to flee in case of danger. "I'd be glad to help you if I can."

"So here's the deal." The president was doing the talking while his chief of staff remained uninvolved. Long ago, the president and his chief had worked out this method of convincing people to help them—the person who couldn't be refused would ask for the favor while the other faded into the background.

"We need someone who is a climate change expert. There is a major conference coming up and we need to send a highly qualified scientist as part of the team that will represent us."

For a second, Malone panicked. *Does the president want me to be that expert? I'm simply not qualified! But if I admit that, then what?* He thought.

Mark's panic showed itself as sweat. Parker saw what was happening. He got up and walked over to where Mark was sitting, pulled up a chair, and sat down.

"Mark, the president is not suggesting that you represent us. He knows that your area of expertise is meteorology and not climate change. He was just seeking a recommendation."

Mark visibly relaxed. "Let me think." He sat there and began to hum the "Thinking Tune."

"Why are you using that tune?" The president's sudden question flustered him.

"What? Huh?" Malone sputtered.

"My tune! You were humming my tune!" the president said with a hint of agitation in his voice.

In a silky smooth voice, Parker came to Malone's rescue. "Mr. President," he purred, "the entire presidential staff hums it now around the White House. I hear it all the time."

The president, though pacified, was still a bit miffed that something so personal had become public property to such a degree that people would hum his tune without any thought. *This is probably how the Lord of Sandwich must have felt when his name became a household word,* the president told himself. Out loud he said with unfelt enthusiasm, "Fine, no problem. Mark, did the tune help?"

He wished it had. He even screwed up his face, trying to remember the name that eluded him but was somewhere in the back of his mind. "I have a name, but I can't think of it just now. Can I get back to you later when I remember?"

The president assured Mark that he could. Then he asked, "Do you think you'd be able to spare any time to go to my son's school tomorrow? He's supposed to make a presentation to his class on the weather and I thought it would be nice if he had a weatherman as qualified as you–"

Mark interrupted before Carl could finish. Carl Jr. had already asked him earlier that day. "No problem. I'll be there. Your secretary will give me the details, right?"

"Yes! Whew! I was worried you'd say you were too busy!"

A knock on the door stopped Mark from replying. He opened the door and saw a staff member standing alongside a tall, black man dressed in a long, flowing, colorful robe and embroidered skull cap. Sadiki Azikiwe might have left the African continent, but the culture and lifestyle had not left him! "Mah mahn!" Azikiwe called to the president, who rose to greet the guest. "How ahr you?" His heavily

Chapter Twenty-Two   141

accented English was endearing to his friends. It gave him an air of sophistication, at least to Americans.

The president gave him a big hug and Azikiwi pounded the president's back with his large hand. "Ouch!" the president complained with a pretend grimace. "Take it easy, will you?"

By this time, others were filing into the room. Malone took advantage of the confusion and made his escape.

CHAPTER TWENTY-THREE

Josh walked slowly up the stamped concrete walkway leading to the Gelbtuchs' home. The wind was blowing on this cold and rainy Friday night, and the thought of eating some of Mrs. Gelbtuch's piping hot chicken soup warmed him. He was glad to see that the lights were on. His visit this week was not expected. Not that Josh was "crashing" the party, but this visit had not been arranged beforehand.

Ever since that first Friday night dinner, Josh had become a regular at Pinny's house. At first Pinny would invite Josh on Wednesday for Friday. Eventually, Mr. Gelbtuch had told Josh that he had a standing invitation at the Friday night *seudah*. Josh took advantage of the warm embrace of a surrogate family and visited at least twice a month. Actually, Josh had been there just last week! But here he was again, making his way up the front steps.

He decided to come because Pinny had not visited his office all week. Although Pinny's visits had decreased some since he no longer needed to sell his candy, Pinny had not come by even once this week.

Josh knocked on the door. He was a little puzzled. Usually, the loud sounds from the busy household blared through the closed door. Some Friday nights, Josh waited before knocking, allowing the lively voices to cheer him. Other Friday nights, Josh stood on the stoop listening to the laughter and pining away for the family life that he did not enjoy as a youth. This week, however, no noise came through the door. Not even the cry of the baby.

Josh knocked again. The door opened slowly, as if Mrs. Gelbtuch was distracted. Looking at her, Josh sensed something was wrong, but could not decipher what it might be. "Good Shabbos, Mrs. Gelbtuch. Is there a problem? Is this a bad week? I could come back some other time if you want." Josh was rambling.

Mrs. Gelbtuch needed a minute to focus, and then she said with her typical congeniality, "Please, Josh, you are part of our family. I insist that you come in! Good Shabbos to you! I'm sorry I looked surprised to see you. It's just that this is the first time that you came to us two weeks in a row."

"Children," Mrs. Gelbtuch called as she handed Josh a hanger for his damp coat, "set a place for Josh at the table!" Turning back to Josh, she hung his coat in the closet and invited him directly into the dining room.

As usual, the table looked exquisite. The silver *becher* filled with dark red wine sparkled and reflected the glow of the Shabbos candles. The white challah cover with the words *lekavod Shabbos* embroidered in gold concealed the still steaming, flavorful challos that Josh looked forward to eating when he came on Friday nights. The family was bedecked in their Shabbos finery and standing appropriately by their seats, awaiting Kiddush.

"I guess I missed '*Shalom Aleichem*,'" Josh joked. The silence was discomfiting. Something was amiss. Then, as if a light bulb suddenly turned on in his head, Josh understood what was wrong. Standing at the head of the table, in place of Mr. Gelbtuch was Mrs. Gelbtuch! She had lifted the cup for Kiddush. And, with a second glance around the table, Josh realized that Pinny was not there either! Also, the children's faces looked cloudy, as if a word could cause a thunderburst bringing torrents of tears.

"Mrs. Gelbtuch," Josh hesitantly asked, "could I ask you something before Kiddush?" Not waiting for a reply, Josh's question exploded from his lips. "Where are they? Is everything all right? What's going on?"

Mrs. Gelbtuch put the *kos* down and sat in her chair. Some of the other kids copied their mother. Chedva was about to answer Josh; she had even opened her mouth to speak, when she remembered the lesson that her *morah* had taught just that week: "So, we see from Lavan that only people who are really lacking in their connection with Hashem answer a question asked to their parents before their parents have a chance to answer. Actually, Rashi comments just at this point that Lavan was a *rasha*. We see that this *middah* of answering before one's parents is a very serious sin."

Mrs. Gelbtuch noticed Chedva's mouth open and close. She gave Chedva a quick smile, as if to say thanks and convey how proud she was of Chedva's self-control. This *middah* of not answering was a challenge for Chedva, and mother and daughter had spent the entire challah-baking time discussing it.

"Well," Mrs. Gelbtuch began as she turned to face the now seated Josh, "my husband and Pinny are in Sinai Hospital—not *chas v'shalom* for a sickness—but in school this week, Pinny got hurt during gym. His arm was severely broken. He was taken to the hospital and admitted. The surgeon and pediatric specialist took their time, but they decided that the surgery that Pinny clearly needed had to happen after a day or two. There needed to be some time for the swelling to subside. We spoke to a Rav who said that as soon as the doctors could do the surgery, they should—even if it involved *chillul Shabbos*—so the surgery was scheduled for today. By the time it began, it was about a half hour until Shabbos. So, while we knew that my husband and Pinny would be in the hospital over Shabbos, we are still very anxious because we do not know how the surgery went or even if it's over yet."

That explains it, thought Josh. *Even though Mrs. Gelbtuch and the children are understandably nervous and worried, they are trying to be brave. Mrs. Gelbtuch is trying to look composed and is working hard to allow the rest of the family to have an authentic Shabbos experience.* Josh was amazed. He very much wanted to help.

"How about if after Kiddush and challah, I go to the hospital and check on things, and then return with a report?" he asked.

Mrs. Gelbtuch was at a loss as to how to respond. She knew that Josh was not *shomer Shabbos*. If she encouraged him to go, he would likely drive, and she and her family would be contributing to his *chillul Shabbos*. Even if Josh did not drive, there were still other issues—like automatic electric doors—he would be faced with once at the hospital. Sinai was user-friendly to those who were *shomer Shabbos*, since it was located in an Orthodox community, but one still had to be aware of what to look out for and what to do. On the other hand, she so desperately wanted to know if everything was okay.

Tzviki came to the rescue. While it never dawned on him that Josh might drive to the hospital, he realized that Josh would not know how to navigate the Shabbos issues of the hospital. Also, although he and Pinny had their share of battles, he loved his brother and wanted to see him.

"Ma," he asked hesitantly, "maybe I could go with Josh, and that way I'd show him the Shabbos entrance and stuff like that?" Tzviki's voice petered out, as he wasn't sure if he had said the right or wrong thing. His mother's reply reassured him.

"That is a great idea!" she said. "I am so proud of you for suggesting it!" Turning to Josh, she asked, "Would it be okay if Tzviki walks with you to Sinai and shows you the special Shabbos path, and door, and the stairs?"

Josh had known that driving was a no-no. He had been planning on walking all along. But he did not know anything about Shabbos rules for the hospital. He also was unsure if Tzviki could walk the four miles, round trip, in the wet weather.

"Do you really think you can do it, Tzviki? It's a long walk and it's cold outside. Even I'm going to find it difficult!"

Tzviki laughed. "Oops. I am not laughing at you, really. You see, my best friend is Chaim Shapiro, who lives on Clarinth. Every Shabbos I walk to his house because, well firstly, he's my friend, but also, his parents are the funniest people, so I like going. I think it's about the same distance as the hospital, wouldn't you say, Ma?"

Mrs. Gelbtuch thought for a little and then nodded yes.

Josh smiled. These kids were great! "Look, if you want to go and your mother lets, you can come. I must admit that along the way you're going to have to explain this whole Shabbos-in-the-hospital thing to me."

Mrs. Gelbtuch gave her approval. Chedva again bit her tongue. She had things to say, but she did not want to join the ranks of Lavan. So, after Kiddush, *hamotzi*, and a piece of fish, Josh and Tzviki bentched. They dressed for the rainy weather and began the forty-five minute trek to see Pinny.

CHAPTER TWENTY-FOUR

Arriving at the hospital cold, but sweaty, Tzviki led Josh through the Blaustein entrance and down the long hallway toward the main lobby. During their walk down Northern Parkway, Tzviki had explained the Shabbos issues to Josh. He pointed out that there was going to be a halachic problem finding Pinny, since it would require asking someone to check a computer. Also, with the updated HIPAA Regulations, visitors asking about patients had to provide both identification and proof of their relationship. Since those documents were *muktzeh*, they were not permitted to handle them on Shabbos. Hearing about the problems, Josh simply replied, "Leave it to me."

Arriving in the main lobby, Tzviki sniffed the air, taking in the sterile, antiseptic scent generic to all medical facilities. He paused near the gift shop, unsure as to exactly where to go. Josh did not break his stride. He made his way to the security desk strategically placed in front of a bank of elevators. Tzviki quickly caught up. A uniformed, elderly man sat on a stool in front of the high desk, watching visitors roam the lobby. Josh stood before him and smiled.

"My name is Josh," Josh said, extending his hand. Grasping the other man's hand, Josh gave a firm shake. "This here is my friend Tzviki. Tzviki's father is here with Tzviki's brother, who is in surgery. We wanted to connect with his dad somehow. Can you help us?"

Josh's polite manners and upbeat attitude made the guard, whose name tag said Leroy Williams on it, feel kindly toward them. Leroy was determined to help these fine folks as much as he could.

"Sure, young man, I can help. How about you just show me some ID and we'll find whoever you are looking for."

"Actually," Josh replied, "that's part of the problem. It's the Sabbath and…"

"Of course, of course. I forgot. Sorry," the guard apologized. "We see a lot of Jewish people here. It's fine." The guard opened a drawer in the desk and pulled out two clip-on visitor's badges. Handing them to Josh, the guard explained, "Usually, we print a sticker badge with your picture on it, but for you, we have these. Now let's see if we can find the person you want. What's the patient's name and what is he here for?"

"Pinny Gelbtuch, for surgery on his arm," Josh answered. "His father is here with him," he added.

"Okay." The guard thought for a moment and began to type into the computer on his desk.

Tzviki spoke suddenly. "Sir? Is it possible to locate them without the computer? You see, since it's the Sabbath…"

"You don't want me to use electronics," the guard finished Tzviki's request. Smiling, he said, "Sure, no problem. Why don't I just send you upstairs to the fourth floor? The surgical center's waiting room is there. Maybe you'll find the boy's father there. If not, you can ask a nurse on that floor for additional help."

Josh asked Mr. Williams to show him the way to the stairs.

"Sabbath again, so no elevator, right?" Williams said, nodding his head knowingly as he pointed to a door marked "Stairs."

Tzviki and Josh nodded and thanked the guard profusely as they quickly headed through the door to begin their climb to the fourth floor.

Once there, Josh and Tzviki opened the door to the hallway and looked around. "There!" Tzviki pointed to a sign hanging from the ceiling. It said "Waiting Room" and had an arrow pointing down the hall to the left.

Josh and Tzviki followed that arrow and the next one, finally arriving at the right place. Entering, they found a room that was designed to create a warm, yet still reassuringly professional ambience to comfort those whose relatives were undergoing surgery. Sconce-shaped lights offered soft white light throughout the room, while lamps were strategically placed near lounge chairs to provide brighter light for reading.

Tall potted plants with large green leaves accented each corner. On the right side of the room, a brown couch hugged the wall, above which hung a large, beautiful painting of flowers. The opposite wall served as host to a mural of fish swimming majestically in the deep sea. Underneath this aquatic wonderland was a small table. Three empty, sculpted gray plastic chairs were snugly tucked in, while the fourth was home to a slumped heap of clothing that concealed the identity of the chair's tenant.

Josh inched toward the slumbering clothes. Tzviki quietly followed. Together they studied the individual's appearance. Black shoes. Suit. Yarmulka. Maybe it was Mr. Gelbtuch, but, then again, Baltimore had a large Jewish community. It was naive to think that only one child was having surgery that day.

Tzviki then spotted the real clue. The head, face down, was resting on an open *Chumash*. Handwritten notes on Rashi decorated its margins. "That's my father's handwriting!" he whispered to Josh.

Josh cleared his throat as he placed his hand on the slumberer's back. "Mr. Gelbtuch?" he said softly.

Mr. Gelbtuch's head shot up. He was expecting the doctor to inform him when Pinny was ready for visitors. He began speaking before turning around. "Yes, doctor, is Pinny–" Turning around, he saw who it was. "My dear friend, Josh! *Zeeskeit*, Tzviki! How good to see you!"

Reaching out, he pulled both of them to him for a group hug. When he let them go, Josh noticed tears glistening in Mr. Gelbtuch's eyes. Josh became apprehensive. "Is everything okay?" he asked fearfully.

"*Baruch Hashem*. Everything is fine. The surgery went well. Don't mind me. I think the tension of the day mixed with the pleasure of seeing you two is getting to me. So, what inspired you make the long trek here? How did you guys link up with each other?"

Together, Josh and Tzviki explained the whole story. Then Tzviki was quiet. It was now time for Josh to present the idea that the two had come up with during their hike.

"You know," Josh said with great feeling, "we had this idea. Your family at home could benefit from your being there and you are probably worn out and hungry. Let us stay here in your place. We could spend the night, and tomorrow you can relieve us."

"Wow!" Mr. Gelbtuch gushed. "That is so very kind! Tzviki, was this your idea?"

Chapter Twenty-Four

Tzviki nodded modestly.

"I am so touched. Josh, you are a really super friend!"

"Well, Mr. Gelbtuch, Pinny means a lot to both of us."

Mr. Gelbtuch started thinking, *I can tell that Josh really wants to stay overnight, and Tzviki would be with him to help with any Shabbos matters.*

Aloud, Mr. Gelbtuch said, "Sounds good to me, but I really want to hear what the doctor thinks about it and ask Pinny too. So–"

A nurse poked her head into the room. "Mr. Gelbtouch," she said, mispronouncing the hard *ch* sound, "your son, Piney, is awake if you want to see him. And the doctor is available to explain to you how the surgery went." She turned and glared at Tzviki.

Tzviki, who had been smirking because of the woman's funny way of saying his last name, now was on the verge of explosive laughter. Tzviki tried to wipe his smile away and swallow the laugh, but he noticed a big grin on his father's face.

"I'll be right there," Mr. Gelbtuch said to distract the nurse from Tzviki's threatened burst of laughter. Turning back to his guests, Mr. Gelbtuch said, "Wait here for a couple of minutes till I return, okay?"

Indignantly, the nurse left the room without a backward glance. Mr. Gelbtuch hurried after her. A few minutes later, he was back. "They are getting ready to move Pinny to his room. I discussed your plan with him and he likes it. So follow me, and I will lead you to Room 612a. We'll be there when Pinny arrives."

CHAPTER TWENTY-FIVE

"Slaves!" The word burst forth from Dmitri Kolyanov's dry lips as he stood watching the barebacked men haul more heavy equipment into the deep, subterranean cavern. "And I am no better than they." Dmitri spat on the ground as if to emphasize his point. He was not really talking to anyone, and in truth, nobody cared what he thought.

Kolyanov was one of the scores of unlucky souls who found themselves stuck at the crossroads of Russia, Kazakhstan, and Mongolia, deep inside the once famous Okladnikov Cave in the

Altai Mountains. Years ago, the skeletal remains of a Neanderthal adolescent was discovered there by Svante Pääbo,[24] casting a spotlight on the cave. After decades of research and excavations, the dark depth of the mountain had no more to offer anthropologists or palaeontologists. They left behind a mess.

The Russian government made a big deal about the damage the international research teams did to the area. This was really a ploy. Under the guise of going in to clean it up, the Russian government moved in with heavy equipment to expand the cave and turn it into an underground base for secret military purposes. Later, the base too, was shut down.

Three years earlier, Kolyanov had been a frustrated nuclear engineer without a job and without any hope for future employment. A poor choice in political ideology had placed his name on the blacklist, despite his outstanding expertise in his field. He had been living on the streets when a black van pulled up next to him and a KGB look-alike jumped out.

"Are you Dmitri Kolyanov, the engineer?" the well-dressed thug demanded. Thoroughly frightened by the man's size and authority, Dmitri had managed to squeak out a timid, "*Da!*"

What followed was a whirlwind of activity. He was escorted forcibly into the car, blindfolded, and carted away to some unknown location—a windowless building somewhere in the capital city.

There, in a locked room, Dmitri sat for two days. There was no food or water, and only a small pail in the corner for bodily needs. Finally, a uniformed man had come in and sat down on a chair that a guard had provided.

"Dmitri," the man had said, sporting a sardonic grin, "you like *svoboda*, freedom, no?"

---

[24] http://www.newscientist.com/article/dn12711-neanderthals-roamed-as-far-as-siberia.html#.VQGJPPnF-So.

Dmitri replied in the affirmative.

"Well, for you, *svoboda* lies in making the correct choice. I need the help of a man with your skills, but it is a *sekretnaya*, a secret, so payment is not possible. I need you to volunteer. You help me and I will keep you free."

At this point, the man's face curled in anger and he threatened Dmitri, "But if you refuse, you will regret it from the *podzemel'ye*, dungeon, of the president!"

Dmitri had chosen to volunteer. Though he had no idea what he was volunteering for, Dmitri had been sure that it would be better than being homeless and unemployed, or worse. Now he had his doubts.

Dmitri had been transported, together with many other coerced volunteers, to the Altai Mountains. These mountains served as home to more than fifty species of mammals and hundreds of species of birds. The flowerful meadows and forests filled with endemic plant life[25] offered the pristine state of nature for which smog-gagging city folk pine. Along the way, the conscripts had gazed out of the open-backed, heavy army transport trucks at the incredible landscape. The beauty caused them to forget, however temporarily, their trepidations concerning the project for which they had been chosen.

All feelings of relief dissipated as soon as the convoy of trucks stopped at the entrance to the cave. Before them, two cages, suspended on massive wooden pulley systems, each big enough to hold ten or more men, hovered over gaping holes. There were soldiers standing around the trucks, with their gun muzzles facing the ground but their fingers hovering near the triggers. Though they were dressed in military uniforms, none of the soldiers wore any insignia or indication as to the branch of military they were serving in or their rank.

---

25 http://www.mapsofworld.com/travel/destinations/russia/golden-mountains-of-altai.

As the backs of the trucks were opened, the men were forced out and ordered to form single-file lines in front of the cages. One man, clearly in charge, announced over the loudspeaker, "Everyone go ten at a time into the elevators. Don't push."

The announcement helped funnel the confused crowd of milling humanity into organized lines by the cages in order to be lowered into the bowels of the earth. However, the proclamation did nothing to solve the intense pushing and shoving that is always present among fearful people waiting for the unknown.

Dmitri waited on line and watched as the first shift of people sank out of sight. His heart palpitated rapidly. *Deep breaths, deep breaths*, he thought again and again. Finally, he heard the loud creaking of the cages' ascent.

"Get in!" The armed men pushed the next group into the cages like sheep herded for the slaughter. Dmitri was in this group. The loud clang of his cage's door and the loud thunk of the bolt sealing the door shut brought panic to many in the carriage. Dmitri kept mentally uttering his mantra: *Deep breaths, deep breaths*.

Upon reaching the bottom, the riders were discharged without ceremony by a command from an unseen source, "*Vi'chadi*—Everybody out!" Before the new arrivals stood a series of booths manned by soldiers. With barks and growls from the soldiers, the men slowly formed new lines in front of each booth. One by one, the recruits passed through the booths.

Finally, it was Dmitri's turn. He walked up to the booth and saw a nondescript man sitting in front of a computer. Without picking up his head to look at Dmitri, the man demanded, "Name?"

"Dmitri Kolyanov."

The soldier scanned his screen, then tapped it a number of times in different spots and said, "You go to the blue building on the left."

Dmitri looked to the left and was amazed to see a three-story building painted in an ugly blue-green color standing in the subterranean space, with hundreds of feet between its roof and the cavern's rocky ceiling.

"Move, foolish man! Don't just gawk. You're holding up the line!" Other, not-so-pleasant words began to ooze out of the soldier's mouth.

The soldier's shouting and increasingly sharp language made Dmitri rush to his destination and open the door without a backward glance. The interior was not much prettier than its shell. White walls stained with dirt and accented by spidery cracks in the plaster were a fine contrast to the pea-soup green, swiss cheese kind of ceiling that appeared to be transported from a war zone. He found himself before a desk sergeant of sorts. The sergeant brought Dmitri to a room that looked like a jail cell and smelled like the reptile house in a zoo. Two worn-out chairs were pulled up to a dilapidated desk.

"Someone will be with you soon." The sergeant walked out of the room, leaving the door open.

Dmitri walked over to one of the chairs. He wiggled it to see if it was sturdy. It was. Dmitri sat down and drummed his fingers on the desk. After a few moments, a stiff-looking soldier carrying a file folder came rushing in and sat down in the empty chair. A second soldier entered the room and remained standing by the doorway.

"We will now conduct a quick job interview," the stiff soldier said in a tired and bored voice.

This job interview was one that Dmitri wished to forget. It began with an embarrassing body search performed by the second soldier, which will not be described, and contained endless questions about his engineering knowledge and skill. The first soldier's silence and lack of emotion as he did his job was eerie.

"All right," Mr. Bored said as he stood to leave. The second soldier had walked out already.

"Hey!" Dmitri said. "What's going on?"

To give the first soldier credit, he did not just ignore Dmitri's request. Instead, he stood holding onto the doorframe and answered most of Dmitri's queries in short, abrupt sentences. When the dust had settled, Dmitri understood the truth. He was now a prisoner. Of whom? That was not clear. Certainly, the impression was that the Russian government was running the operation, though there were some things that indicated differently.

Dmitri was charged with the task of overseeing the creation of a massive nuclear propulsion system of unimaginable size and proportion. At his disposal, he had teams of other scientists, electronic experts, propulsion experts, and hundreds of criminals who traded prison time for years of heavy labor below the earth's surface.

All the details of the project were eventually presented to him. Dmitri was told, "The Office expects you to..." or "The Office demands that you include..." Dmitri just followed the orders. Only if he thought that the plans issued from up high would make the project fail did Dmitri offer his opinion to the messenger. The messenger appeared to deliver what he said back to "the Office," because, in such cases, they would issue a new directive that was identical to what Dmitri had suggested.

So, after five years, Dmitri was standing on a platform from where he could see a large number of the workers, musing and cursing his luck. Dmitri had come to this spot many times over the years and relived the beginning of this nightmare. Each time, he had tried to think of a way he could have escaped the goon from the car or made a surreptitious exit from this awful place without getting shot. His hunch, which would be confirmed or denied shortly, now that the project was basically completed, was that no one who worked on this system would ever see daylight again.

Dmitri let his gaze travel along what they had built—a huge, camouflaged cylinder. It was massive. Painted on its side in gigantic

Cyrillic letters was the name of this mammoth: *Podarok*, The Gift. Inside its tubular case, The Gift housed the largest nuclear thermal propulsion system on Earth. The entire unit was made up of separately crafted, but merged stages, mounted on hydraulic lifts that were able to send the tube's nozzle many stories above the top of the mountain. It was fitted with an ingenuous mechanism that allowed the cap of the mountain to split in half and then retract, permitting the unit to rise out of its crater like a dragon rising out of its lair. At the same time, the mountaintop fit snugly around the tube, using Earth's natural density to protect the cylinder from vibrating when it was activated.

The hefting of the equipment that Dmitri was currently overseeing was just cleanup that had been ordered from the people at the top. Machinery and tools that were not in use were being removed for storage in another location.

"Dmitri?"

Dmitri looked around. Coming toward him was his assistant, Ivan Ivankopf. *"Da?"*

"Dmitri, my friend, I heard they are coming to take us home soon. Did you hear that? Soon we will be free!" Ivan was especially happy. His life sentence for various political crimes had been shortened by his use of scientific expertise to help Mother Russia.

Dmitri rolled his eyes. "Ivan, I told you a thousand times, don't count your chickens before they hatch. I'm not even sure that the whole thing will work!"

"Why?" Ivan asked with a twinkle in his eyes. "Did they get the parts from Amazon.com?"

"Actually, they did," Dmitri replied with a smile.

They continued their banter back and forth for a few minutes. Then Dmitri noticed the masked men.

Chapter Twenty-Five

CHAPTER TWENTY-SIX

"Exquisite! I'm so glad that the taxpayers' dollars are being used for a master chef in the White House." Sam Woodrop was impressed with the cuisine. The six-course dinner matched up to, and perhaps exceeded, the flavorful food in Blanca, the upscale restaurant in Manhattan's Lower East Side. Not only was the food good, the conversation between Sam and Kara and the president and his wife flowed seamlessly from one topic to another. Politics was not at all part of the discussion, and for a White House dinner hosting a wealthy man, that was unusual.

This free exchange of opinions and ideas, and the relaxed atmosphere, underscored the deeper friendship of the Almond and Woodrop families. Though there were other guests in the room, the president and his wife had a private table with Sam and Kara.

"Sam, I need some advice. You see, Secretary Parker has reminded me that the United States needs to send representatives to the GCGW pretty soon, and I need a climate change expert to lead the group. Now, I know that saving the planet is your thing. Do you know of anyone who could help us out?"

The president had thought about this question all night. He needed an expert, but he grappled with asking for Sam's recommendation. Sam had some pretty wacky ideas sometimes. However, Sam and Kara had access to the country's best people in the field of global warming—thanks to their generous contributions—and therefore were most likely to know the right expert.

Sam looked a bit startled at the president's words. He quickly recovered and cleared his throat. Sam scratched his right ear and then began to stroke his clean-shaven chin. "I have an idea of someone who might be good. I am not sure how much experience he has in politics or even with the climate change community, but I was very impressed with his knowledge and his character. I heard him speak at the University of Maryland one weekend and I even began to do some research into his company, since he had written, asking me to help back him financially." Sam paused. He sipped some of his Asti before continuing, "I was impressed with what I read. Now I have to remember his name. I have it on my computer at work, but..."

Sam turned to his wife. "Kara?"

Kara was busy laughing after listening to the latest White House tale about Carl Jr. "Sam, you must hear this story." Caught up in her own desire to speak, she missed her husband's attempt to communicate.

"Kara, I am so sorry, but first could I ask you," Sam smoothly interjected, "what was the name of that speaker at the university reunion who spoke about climate changes?"

"Oh! You mean the fellow who carried our suitcase?" Kara asked. "I think Josh something...actually, didn't you scan his card into your phone?"

"Right!" Sam took out his cell phone and let his fingers flit across its screen. Seconds later he looked up at the president. "Joshua Green, Assistant Professor at UMBC. I even have his number. Shall we call him?"

CHAPTER TWENTY-SEVEN

"Calm down, Mrs. Gelbtuch," the doctor urged. "Try to tell me why you've brought Pinny to the ER this evening."

Mrs. Gelbtuch took a deep breath and tried to speak without seeming anxious. Like a neon sign, her face flashed her feelings of worry. She was feeling flushed. Sweat was beading up on her forehead in the air-conditioned room. She began to speak, hoping she could explain everything clearly for the doctor.

"As I said, my son had surgery here a couple of weeks ago. Since then, Pinny has been doing pretty well. He went back to school, and although he has a cast, things mostly went back to normal.

"Then, yesterday morning, Pinny woke up with a fever of 101°F, so he stayed home from school and spent most of the day sleeping. We knew that Pinny had been around boys in school who were sick. That, and the fact that he had a runny nose and sore throat the night before, made us think it was a virus of some sort.

"We checked his arm some time during the day, but didn't see anything unusual. After his surgery, we had been told to come right back if a fever developed within the next ten days, but this is well past that time frame.

"Well, a few hours ago, my husband went to help Pinny move from the couch, where he had fallen asleep, to his bed. My husband placed his hands on Pinny's shoulders to guide him toward his bedroom and Pinny screamed so loud that a couple of the kids woke up! Pinny then dropped to the floor and lay writhing in pain. My husband carefully unbuttoned his shirt, removed Pinny's sleeve, and saw that his arm was now discolored and very swollen around the cast. It looked awful! So we rushed right over here and have been waiting to see you."

Doctor Neil Wills, the orthopedic surgeon on call, gently touched the dark red area on Pinny's arm. He had cut off the cast in order to get a better look at it. Now that he saw the full degree of the swelling and the discoloration, he knew that in all likelihood Pinny had an SSI, a surgical site infection.

Not ready to say for sure just yet, Dr. Wills uttered in a sagely tone, "This area feels very hot. Clearly it hurts a lot. Ah, here are the ultrasound pictures I ordered."

Wills looked at the computer images for a full minute without making a sound. Chana Gelbtuch was growing frantic as she watched the doctor's eyes squint and flitter with concern.

Unable to contain herself, she exploded, "What?! What's wrong?"

Dr. Wills replied grimly, "It's like I thought. We need to admit Pinny back into the hospital. He has an infection that requires an infusion of strong antibiotics, and possibly I will need to go in and clean out the area of the break. But that would have to be after some of the swelling subsides."

Pinny, who had been quiet until now, groaned loudly and whispered something. His mother leaned over. "Pinny, my dear, say it again. What? What do you want me to tell the doctor?"

This time, Pinny's pained and shaky voice was a bit louder as he said, with hot tears dripping down his cheeks and losing themselves on the pillow under his head, "The class trip is on Sunday!"

"What was that?" asked Dr. Wills.

"Oy. My dear son," Mrs. Gelbtuch sighed deeply and sympathetically. To the doctor she said, "Pinny's class is going to Philadelphia on Sunday, and he worked really hard to earn the money to pay for this trip. He's been looking forward to it for a while now, and he's understandably upset that he won't be going."

The doctor made some clucking sounds before he typed up his notes and completed the necessary forms to arrange for Pinny's hospital stay. They were supposed to express sympathy, but fell short. Even his distracted words of "I'm sorry this happened to you, Pinny," came off sounding flat.

✦

Sitting in his office back at school, Rabbi Fried listened to the voice on the other end of the phone line while gazing with pleasure at the photographs on the wall. While his main responsibility was serving as the fourth-grade *rebbi*, he had also been given the responsibility of arranging and chaperoning the eighth graders on their graduation trip.

As a token of appreciation for his efforts, his first-ever eighth grade charges had presented Rabbi Fried with a framed group picture of them posing around a little-known statue of the great statesman Benjamin Franklin that was tucked away in a small park in Philadelphia. Thus a tradition was born, and the subsequent classes did the same. The spot where the eight pictures now hung became known as "The Wall of Fame." Not every picture was exactly the same. Some years, the boys would rest their hands on the statue's shoulders, other times they made bunny ears with their fingers behind Franklin's head. Once, the entire class stood while wearing "Early to bed and early to rise... and you'll look like me!" T-shirts along with Benjamin Franklin wigs (with shoulder length hair flowing around a bald crown) that they had bought at one of the souvenir shops.

Rabbi Fried was an efficient and well-groomed man. His salt-and-pepper beard falsely bespoke his young thirty-three years of age and his athletic ability. He was the *rebbi* who challenged *talmidim* to games on the basketball court—and won! The students loved their trip to Philadelphia with Rabbi Fried as one of the chaperones. They knew that everywhere they went would automatically be fun! The students also knew that Rabbi Fried was honest and fair, and so they were willing to tell him about things that went on among the students that they would not say to another *rebbi*, let alone the *menahel*.

"Yes, Mrs. Gelbtuch...Uh huh...Oy, that's terrible! Is there anything I can...No! I understand...For sure! A full refund!"

Rabbi Finegold knocked on the doorpost and indicated that he wished to enter the office.

"Listen, Mrs. Gelbtuch, we will take care of everything as soon as you have the time. Uh, I'm sorry to have to cut this conversation short, but I have someone here waiting for me, so I must go. But if you have any other issues or need any help, feel...Yes, I will tell Rabbi Finegold..."

Hearing his name and seeing Rabbi Fried's welcoming nod, the *menahel* entered the room and raised his eyebrows inquiringly. Rabbi Fried raised one finger, indicating that he would explain in a minute.

Rabbi Finegold sat down in the dark-gray plastic chair across from Rabbi Fried. He reached over, and after a slight nod of permission from the *rebbi*, he took a Laffy Taffy from the ever-present big bowl of candy on Rabbi Fried's desk. He unwrapped it and popped it into his mouth.

"Okay, so *zai gezunt* and tell Pinny that we are wishing him a big *refuah sheleimah*! Goodbye." Rabbi Fried hung up the phone.

"Pinny is sick?" Rabbi Finegold asked while trying to remove the gooey candy from his teeth.

"Worse! His arm, you know, where he had the surgery? It's infected! His mother took him to the hospital. He will be there for at least a few days. Possibly, he will need another operation! His mother called to tell me that there is no way that Pinny will be joining us on Sunday's trip to Philadelphia."

Rabbi Finegold's heart was filled with compassion. Pinny had really matured in his learning and *middos tovos* since his bar mitzvah, and it was sad that he was suffering from the pain of his infected arm and missing what promised to be a great trip. "Oy. That is really awful, especially after he was so proud that he raised the money for the trip himself. I hope that Hashem sends him a speedy *refuah* through the right *shaliach*." The *menahel* continued, "I'll tell the boys to say *Tehillim* for him after Minchah. Good idea, no?"

Rabbi Fried hesitated for a minute before replying. He was debating with himself about something. When he did speak up, it was in such a quiet voice that the *menahel* had to lean toward him to hear.

"You know," Rabbi Fried began, "there has been talk among the boys that maybe the collision was not by mistake. There was talk that something was going on between the two boys who were involved…"

Chapter Twenty-Seven

Rabbi Fried had already said more than he knew. The rumors were just that—rumors. He felt that there was definitely something that led up to "The Hockey Crash," as the students called it. No one had actually said with certainty that Eli Truxenberg had been bullying Pinny, and even with his snooping around, the matter was still murky. But the talk was that Eli was bothering Pinny, and Rabbi Fried saw that some students were now avoiding Eli and his clique.

Rabbi Finegold cleared his throat. "I'm aware of some turmoil and I've spent some time investigating the matter. I actually sensed that something was amiss when I first got to the scene of what everyone's calling 'The Hockey Crash.' (Rabbi Finegold was up on the lingo too.) But it is not a *pashut* matter. I still don't have a clear picture of what was going on and I didn't find any real evidence of wrongdoing, although there were indicators that Eli was acting aggressively toward Pinny. I brought it up with Eli, but I just didn't get anywhere, and Pinny did not offer me anything I could work with either.

"I felt I needed advice, so I spoke to my Rav about it. He said that," Rabbi Finegold began to recount the Rav's decision using his thumb and the classic Talmudic study singsong melody, "since sometimes we label kids in a way that could harm them, *and* any action we take could mess up this boy's life as he begins in the Mesivta, *plus* the fact that we are now at the end of June, I should take a more reserved, hands-off approach. The Rav recommended that, for now, I should not do anything. He suggested that I keep close tabs on Eli when he continues in our Mesivta next year. If there is anything that takes place involving Eli that even has a hint of his bullying others, we have halachic grounds to take an aggressive approach—even without hard evidence—in dealing with the bullying behavior."

Agitated, because he understood what it felt like to be bullied, Rabbi Fried stood up and harshly grabbed a folder from the window sill behind his desk. He shrugged his shoulders and said, "Fine.

You're in charge. Now, I'm off to tell the eighth grade that Pinny won't be joining them. Did you want any more nosh?"

If Rabbi Finegold noticed that Rabbi Fried was upset, he did not comment. He nodded his head as he reached forward and took a second Laffy Taffy.

Without comment, an upset Rabbi Fried left the office.

CHAPTER TWENTY-EIGHT

Josh stood in line waiting for his turn to board the plane and looked in amazement at the number of people who would be spending the next eighteen hours together with him in the small traveling village in the sky. He was dressed the part of a dignitary. He wore a dark suit, brand new shiny black oxfords, and a yellow and black paisley tie. Josh held onto his carry-on luggage tightly. Besides his toiletries, his bag held his laptop, as well as a thick binder full of protocols and guidelines for serving as a member of the SEE and representative of the president of the United States.

"Josh?" Pinny asked in a quiet voice.

Josh turned slightly to face his travel companion. Pinny was not coming to Greece in any official capacity. He was with Josh simply to keep Josh company—and to have some fun during his summer vacation!

The idea for Pinny's trip to Athens began soon after he missed the class trip. Pinny was understandably upset. He had raised so much money and had been looking forward to this special trip all year! His parents had offered that Pinny could take a special trip to California or some other location. Their only caveat was that other members of the greater Gelbtuch family reside in the vacation destination. And his parents even offered that one of them would take some time off from work and spend a few days in Philadelphia with him, following the class's itinerary.

But Pinny was simply not interested. His words of refusal about California were, "I don't want to go on a boring trip to be with relatives I don't really know." (In teenage language that means no.)

A new plan was suggested one Friday night. As had become quite common, Josh came over for the *seudah*. After a beautiful rendition of "*Tzur Mishelo*," the conversation turned to examples of *hashgachah pratis* in their lives. Mr. Gelbtuch had just told his *hashgachah* story.

"You see," he said, "Mrs. Gelbtuch lost her car keys, and so, on Tuesday, I made a copy of my keys for her during my lunch break. I intended to give them to my wife at the end of the day. To keep them safe until I got home, I placed them in my wallet. Later, Chana called and said that she had found her keys. By the time I got home from work, there wasn't any need to take them out of my wallet, so I left them there and forgot about them.

"On Thursday, I left my office to drive to a dentist appointment and I couldn't find my keys! I searched my pockets," Mr. Gelbtuch lowered his voice and whispered to his audience in a conspiratorial voice, "and as you know, I have so many of them! I checked them over and over again for like, ten minutes. It always takes me a long time to find things in my pockets."

Everyone laughed. It was so true! The amount of time that Mr. Gelbtuch spent searching his pockets was legendary.

"Anyway, I discovered that I had locked them in the car! Boy, was I frustrated! I called my wife to see if she could get in touch with the dentist and tell him that I had to wait for AAA to send a locksmith.

"Chana then reminded me that I had a copy of the keys in my wallet! So I cancelled the call to AAA and had my teeth checked at the dentist's a short while later! The fact that I had made spare keys for my wife was Hashem's plan so that I would have them when I needed them. That's *hashgachah*!" Mr. Gelbtuch concluded.

This story was followed by a flurry of examples from each of the children. Every incident prompted comments ranging from disbelief to wonder. There were also numerous debates about whether a specific story fell into the *hashgachah pratis* category. The volume in the dining room reached levels only heard in school cafeterias during lunchtime.

Josh had been sitting quietly and listening carefully to each example. The concept of Divine Providence was new to him, but he understood it from all the stories. Josh cleared his throat loudly. The din abruptly subsided.

"I have a weird story that I wanted to share anyway, but I think that this fits in with what you are discussing. You know, a while ago, I was asked to fill in at the university for a professor who was in the hospital. Although I had the day off, I agreed to help out a friend, and besides, I needed the money. The topic of the talk I was supposed to give was one of my favorites—climate change—and I also knew that Sam Woodrop, a famous philanthropist and Save the Planet activist would be there. He also happens to be a personal friend of the president, Carl Almond. Well, Mr. Woodrop liked my speech and complimented me. He even asked me for my business card. When I gave it to him, I got up the nerve to also include another card that I had for my private work on climate issues.

"Some time after my speech, the president asked Mr. Woodrop to recommend an expert on climate change to join the team representing the US at the international Global Conference on Global Warming, and my name came up."

Exclamations issued forth from the children, one after the other.

"Yeah! That's exactly it! That's *hashgachah*!" said one.

"Woodrop, the rich guy? In science class, we read an interview he gave about global warming!" Chedva exclaimed.

Josh raised his hand to stop the ruckus. "Wait! My story isn't over yet. Just listen!"

His eager crowd quieted down and Josh continued, "Last year, when there was the big storm—you know, when I first met Pinny—I had sent my weather predictions to different weather reporters. Most ignored them and were later embarrassed by the incredible inaccuracies of their own forecasts. Only one, Mark Malone from WBAL, paid any attention to what I was saying. I knew this because he broadcast a weather forecast that was identical to mine, while all the other stations were way off, and I knew there was no way he could come up with the exact same conclusions himself. As it turned out, the president gave him a citation for 'his' predictions!"

"What's a site station?" asked little Moishe, causing everyone to laugh.

"*Zeeskeit*, it's a special prize," Mrs. Gelbtuch said to her son.

Josh continued with his story, "I was actually upset at the time because this weatherman did not give me any credit whatsoever. I was at a real low in financing my climate change research, and I thought that if everyone knew that I was the only one who had forecast the storm correctly, I would receive more donations to fund my studies."

A little light bulb went on in Pinny's head. "So that's why you were so upset that time after the storm?"

Josh looked down for a few seconds and shrugged his shoulders. Then he resumed speaking, "Well, after the storm, Mark Malone impressed the governor so much that he became his staff meteorologist. When Almond became president, Malone was appointed the White House's expert meteorologist."

"I don't get what this has to do with you," Chedva said. "Where's the *hashgachah*?"

Pinny snapped at Chedva, "Don't interrupt. Let Josh finish!"

"I'm getting to the point," Josh continued. "It seems that after Woodrop recommended me, the president asked Malone if he had ever heard of me. Malone didn't tell the president about my storm predictions while he was still governor, but he did say that he knew of me and thought that I was very good at what I do.

"So a couple of weeks ago, I was invited to the Oval Office for an interview with the president of the United States! He asked me a lot of questions about all kinds of things."

"Was it cool?" Tzviki asked eagerly.

"Is the Oval Office really an oval?" Pinny asked.

"Yes and yes. But the real kicker is coming. When the president asked me to join the team representing the US at the international conference in Athens, I just couldn't say no. I mean, I was being offered to work for the president himself! What a privilege! The president shook hands with me and said that he was happy I was joining the team of others who would be attending.

"As I was about to leave, he said that the attendees would be meeting with him before we left in order to discuss the United State's official position on various issues. 'And feel free to bring along a friend to do some sightseeing with you when the conference is over!' the president added. Of course, I thought of Pinny. Is that *hashishga pratos*, or whatever it's called?"

For a minute there was a stunned silence. The story's multiple details were unbelievable! Then the floodgates opened and everyone started talking. Mr. Gelbtuch commented that the *hashgachah* was so clear that this story could be written in one of those books about Divine Providence! Mrs. Gelbtuch asked Josh when he was scheduled to leave. The kids were squealing with delight that they knew someone who was going to work for the president of the United States.

Only Pinny was quiet. His chin was resting on his hand and his brows were furrowed. Clearly, he was thinking intensely.

Suddenly, Pinny spoke to his parents, his words bringing order to the chaos. "I want to go." A short sentence made of very simple words, words that would bring angst to any child's parents. Four syllables that pit a child's will against the will of his parents.

Almost at once, both Mr. and Mrs. Gelbtuch said no.

"Why not?" asked Pinny.

Parents often have a gut reaction to an idea that seems wrong. Even though they are not always able to articulate the reason for their negative response, parents have a sixth sense concerning the safety—both spiritually and physically—of their children. The Gelbtuchs did not yet have a clear reason why Pinny could not go. They had not had enough time to think about it. So now they each came up with different excuses.

"You don't have a passport!" Mr. Gelbtuch explained quickly.

"It's not the best place for a religious person to be," Mrs. Gelbtuch said with conviction.

Pinny's set mouth and scrunched up eyebrows showed his parents that they were going to have a great battle on their hands. However, to Pinny's credit, he did not continue at this time.

His parents were both impressed that Pinny had the maturity to hold off on the arguing until later. "I see you are upset, Pinny," his mother said. "I'm proud of you for the good *middos* and *derech eretz* you are displaying now. How about we discuss things after Shabbos?"

Pinny nodded his head, but he was not any happier.

Josh squirmed uncomfortably. "I am so sorry this is causing trouble. I didn't mean for it to."

Mr. Gelbtuch recovered the moment. "Don't worry. This is part of the joy of raising children!" In an attempt to distract Josh from feeling badly, Mr. Gelbtuch turned to his wife. "*Nu*, Chanaleh. Any dessert? Maybe we'll sing a *zemer* while you serve."

Minutes later, there was only one clue as to the impending battle: Pinny's dark face.

❖

It was only on Sunday that Josh called Mr. Gelbtuch and discussed the real possibility of Pinny joining the trip. "After all, he missed his class trip, and I know there will be a few expenses that are beyond the official travel allowance offered by the government, but I really would love to pay for those incidentals. Call it a belated bar-mitzvah present."

Pinny's parents called Rabbi Finegold to discuss the matter. Very surprisingly, Rabbi Finegold thought that it would be a fine idea for Pinny. "He is a strong young man and I am not worried about him. As a matter of fact, based on what you are telling me, I think this fellow Josh might even become observant as a result of Pinny's influence!"

Rav Briskman, Rav of Mishkan Tefillah, the shul that the Gelbtuch family attended, was also consulted. Initially, Rav Briskman was concerned about kosher food and minyanim for Pinny. After some discussion, the Rav called the Rabbi of Thessaloniki, Rabbi Menachem Cooperman. Rabbi Cooperman told him that there was a Sephardi shul called Synagogue Beth Shalom located not far from where the conference was taking place. They had regular minyanim that would follow a different *nusach* than Pinny was used to, but it was a viable option. The rabbi urged Rav Briskman to inform Pinny that security around the shul was strict and visitors needed to bring identification.

"On Shabbos too?" Rav Briskman asked.

"They have a special system arranged with the hotels in the area," Rabbi Cooperman replied. "A valet carries copies of passports to shul for any guest who registered to attend the minyanim. It is all done according to halachah."

Rabbi Cooperman ended the conversation by confirming that kosher food was available and that plenty of Orthodox Jews came to Athens. With these reassurances, Rav Briskman called Pinny's father and gave the green light for Pinny to go.

So that's how Pinny was now waiting in line with Josh for the first flight in his life—to Athens, Greece.

❖

Pinny again called for Josh's attention. There was an urgency in his voice. "What's the matter?" Josh asked his charge in a stage whisper.

"I need to use the restroom. Can I go now? Will we be getting on the plane soon?"

"Nah. There's still time. The bathroom is right over there. Go and come right back."

Josh was happy that this was Pinny's only problem. He had been worried that Pinny would be afraid to fly, but so far, Pinny was just plain excited.

Pinny then ran to the nearby restroom. Minutes later, he came out and started walking back to his spot in line. While muttering an *Asher Yatzar*, Pinny made his way along the side of the long line of people waiting to board the plane. Once he finished with his *berachah*, he engaged in a game of people-watching. He tried to guess why they were flying and what sort of people they were.

Abruptly, he stopped.

Him? Here? What in the world? Uh-oh! What do I do now? Pinny thought in a panic. There, standing before him, only a few spots behind Josh, was the scourge of Pinny's life, the bane of his existence, Eli Truxenberg. "Why is he going to be on this flight, and who is that yarmulka-wearing, clean-shaven, distracted man talking rapidly into his cell phone, standing next to him?"

At that moment, Eli turned around and his eyes met Pinny's stare. A cruel smile curled on his lips. Clearly, the damage he had done to Pinny's arm and the pain he had induced by indirectly forcing Pinny to miss the class trip did nothing to curb Eli's enthusiasm for bringing misery into Pinny's life.

Pinny raced back to his place in line with Josh and said forcefully, "Josh? I saw another couple of Orthodox people behind us. One is a kid I know from school by the name of Truxenberg. Do you know anything about them?"

Just then, the line began to move and, one by one, people boarded the plane and headed toward their assigned seats. "Let's talk about this after we're settled. Remember, our seats are in row 31, seats A and B." Josh grabbed his carry-on and began to move with the line. Pinny did the same.

Twenty minutes later, the pair was seated. Other passengers were still shuffling by, inches at a time. Josh placed his carry-on in an overhead bin and helped Pinny do the same. As he straightened in his seat, Josh commented, "They say that in the Airbus A340, which is this plane, these are not the quietest seats, but when I booked the tickets, I chose seats that I thought would allow you the best view of the outside."

Josh breathed deeply, stretched his legs, at least as far as the cramped space permitted, clasped his hands behind his head, and said, "Now what did you ask me back in line?"

"I saw a classmate of mine and I was..." Pinny stopped talking. He watched as Eli and the man with him walked past where he and Josh were sitting. Eli seemed not to notice Pinny. Josh followed Pinny's gaze.

"That man and boy? Is that your question?"

Pinny just nodded.

"Mr. Richard Truxenberg. I believe that is his son. Richard is the administrative head of the United States Global Research Program, which represents thirteen different government agencies involved in studying aspects of global warming. Officially, we are partners in this conference as representatives of the United States. So, the kid's your friend?"

Pinny shrugged his shoulders. He had no good response so he said, "Not really, but I know him." Pinny glanced back to where Eli had just settled down. Eli was watching him. His balled fist indicated that the bully in him had come along for the ride.

CHAPTER TWENTY-NINE

"Ah, Athens," Dmitri said as he gazed out of the window at the passing scenery. He noticed a cloudy sky, unusual for Athens at this time of year. But then again, weather around the world had changed with the globe's warming. He sat back in his seat in the limousine and tried to ignore his somber, stoic, and rigid companion. Dmitri scratched his legs. The itchy, stiff, black wool suit pants and heavily starched cotton shirt looked nice and cost a dear sum in Russia, but for a man who generally wore jeans and a heavy flannel shirt, the attire was uncomfortable.

Dmitri was willing to suffer some discomfort away from the dark tunnels in the mountain range. Secretly, he would have been willing to do almost anything to get away from his home of five years. He had his suspicions about what had happened to the others involved in the project, and if he was right, then he was perhaps the only one left who could enjoy life.

When the masked men appeared out of nowhere, Dmitri was sure that there would be a lot of shooting—a massacre. But he did not get to see it. One of the guards ran up to him and commanded that he speak to the people in the Office.

Dmitri's expertise and desire to do things properly led the people in charge to respect and trust him to a degree, and they assigned him the mission that brought him to Athens. But the trust was not complete. The soldier sitting next to him was there to make sure that things went smoothly.

Dmitri caught a glimpse of the Acropolis, high in the mountains. He hoped that this would not be the only opportunity for him to do some sightseeing. He wished to see the famous marble Panathinaic Stadium that was built in 566 BCE. He had heard there was a famous chair to sit in that would make for a great photograph to send back home. *Home. Where was that? Where would it be?* Alas, Dmitri had no time to think about these matters now. He needed to focus on the mission at hand. He began to review in his mind the actions being demanded of him by the Office. Dmitri was confident that he was as prepared as he could be.

The white limousine rolled along a lengthy driveway before stopping. "We are here," the driver barked. "This is the Zappeion Exhibition Hall."

As they walked up the long walkway toward the exhibition hall, Dmitri's eyes beheld the famous building. "*Chudesnaya*,"[26] he uttered.

---

26   Magnificent.

It was the only word Dmitri could think of to describe this edifice. Two rows of majestic marble pillars supported the tall entranceway in the center of a long, square-shaped building full of tall windows. In front of the building, a garden of multicolored flowers surrounding a dazzling fountain display practically begged Zappeion guests to stroll there and enjoy the fragrance. Dmitri wished to heed the call, but there was no time to dawdle. Dmitri and the soldier—Dmitri thought his name was Yuri—walked swiftly toward the entrance to the building.

Registering at the Welcome Desk was interesting. Most of the people who attended this conference were scientists and held the title of Doctor, but Dmitri, who was an engineer, and his team of one, were simply listed as observers. However, he saw that there was another group of scientists from the Office attending as representatives of the Russian government. So as they all waited their turn, Dmitri and his shadow overheard scientific chatter in thirty-five different languages. Even had it been in their mother tongue, the pair would not have understood anything.

"Welcome to the conference," a man behind the Welcome Desk said to them in English. "Your names?"

"Dmitri Kolyanov," Dmitri answered.

"Yuri Volkovskn," Dmitri's shadow replied.

"Ah...yes. I see your names here. Okay. Would you like a translator chip? This microchip is inserted just below the skin behind your ear and, once activated, enables you to hear anything said in the language of your choice."

Dmitri glanced at Yuri, who shrugged his shoulders. "Sure. We'll take one each for translation into Russian."

The fellow opened a drawer under the desk and withdrew two pins. "At the tip here is the chip," the man explained. "You will feel a pinch behind your ear as I insert the chip under your skin. Then you will hear all other languages in Russian. This will only be activated during the presentations, and the chip is dissolvable, so it will disappear after forty-eight hours.

"Delegates are gathering for a wine and cheese tasting in Meeting Hall 17," the man continued after pricking their ears. "We have staff throughout the building who can guide you there."

Dmitri enjoyed a glass of Echezeaux, a delicious and expensive Pinot Noir wine, with a piece of exquisite Chèvre, goat cheese, before he and his sidekick made their way into the main presentation hall. It was massive and awe-inspiring. The room was circular and domed. It had the capacity to hold more than one thousand people on the main floor level. All around the room were marble pillars supporting a balcony and more columns from the balcony supporting the roof. In the middle of the room was a raised platform slowly rotating 360 degrees. The one thousand chairs were for the scientists representing the most important nations. Other attendees would either stand in the back of the room or observe the goings-on from the balcony. There was a buzz of excitement in the room, typical of such international gatherings.

People-watching in a crowd such as this was really interesting. The colors of dress stretched from one end of the color spectrum to the other, as did the style of clothes. Dmitri's clothing was bland compared to most. The only flashy part of his wardrobe was the yellow carnation that he was told he must wear. Had Dmitri understood even a handful of the plethora of languages being spoken, he was sure he would have enjoyed his observing even more. But the chip was not yet activated. Dmitri was smiling at the scene before him when he felt a hand grab his upper arm and squeeze tightly. Pain shot through his arm.

"Hello, my friend." The nondescript man who uttered this greeting handed Dmitri a small piece of paper and whispered hastily, "Check the note." Out loud he continued, "I have not seen you in such a long time. I hope your English is not too rusty."

Dmitri was nervous. He almost clammed up. After all, he was an engineer and not a spy! But one look from his soldier friend was enough to remind him to be tough now rather than to suffer later. "I khav been practicing for this meeting," Dmitri said in an exaggerated Russian accent. In better English, he said, "And you, my friend, how have you been?"

"Well, thank you." With those words, the stranger lifted his arm in greeting to another delegate. "Stephan, *wei geht es dir*?"[27] Turning back to Dmitri, he said with a wink, "Time to move on to my next friend."

---

27   German for "How are you?"

CHAPTER THIRTY

Pinny could scarcely believe it. "Josh? Did you see that Jewish cemetery we passed? I never realized that there were Jews in this city so long ago!"

Josh finished attaching his name tag to his jacket and began to fumble with Pinny's. "I'm surprised at you, Pinny. Even *I* know that the Chanukah story took place with the Greeks. Come. Let's check things out!"

Pinny and Josh navigated their way to Hall 17 and entered the crowded room. Josh had made it clear to Pinny that he must stay by his side.

In addition, Pinny had a cell phone to use in the event of an emergency. Now Josh whispered, "Remember! The food is not kosher!"

Pinny was pumped! Food was the furthest thing from his mind. This trip was the coolest ever. Way better than Philly. Pinny looked in the bag of promotional items he had received at the Welcome Desk. It had gizmos and squash balls with logos from tons of companies trying to attract business through their environmental positions. As a "student delegate," Pinny's official title, he was allowed to take refreshments for free from the coffee room and attend any session he wished. Of course, he could only take certain packaged items or fruit, since the rest was probably not kosher. The hotel room that he was encamped in had a Jacuzzi and an electronic everything. The previous night, Pinny had just climbed into bed, and the lights in the room automatically had dimmed on their own!

Across the room, Pinny saw that Eli also had a bag of stuff and was looking around. Pinny thought he looked a little sad. *Hopefully, I won't have to talk to him. If I avoid him, everything will be okay,* Pinny thought.

Pinny followed Josh into Hall 17. The minute he entered the room, Pinny laughed out loud. It looked like his school auditorium on the night of the science fair. There were many booths set up. Some displayed complicated drawings and diagrams on presentation boards, while others exhibited 3-D models. Each represented a scientific organization or an individual hoping to convince delegates to vote in favor of using their ideas to solve global warming.

Josh and Pinny spent a few hours looking at the exhibits. A number of times, they crossed paths with Mr. Truxenberg and his son. It was at the last one of those encounters that Eli's mean streak reared its ugly head.

Pinny was staring in wonder at a display of an idea from a company founded by the billionaire family of Bill Gates, the cofounder of

Microsoft. This plan called for a seawater-spraying machine that could prevent climate change.[28] Big ships with massive spouts would suck up ten tons of water a second and spray it three thousand feet into the air. This would increase cloud density and help block out the dangerous sunlight. The display was a miniature working model that consisted of two ships floating in a pool of water that was sitting on the floor of the room. The three-foot-tall spouts sprayed water five feet into the air, where a heating system turned the mist into a fog. Eventually, the fog turned into droplets and fell back into the pool.

As Pinny stood there watching together with a small crowd, he heard someone whisper into his ear, "I didn't realize my fun would continue into the summer!" Pinny then felt a hand push him forward. As Pinny began to fall into the pool, he sent his hands forward to break his fall. Inadvertently, his hand hit one of the ships. The ship tilted on its side sending a geyser of water into the crowd, soaking many delegates!

The explosion of languages was melodious!

"*Mama mia!*"

"*Aman tanr'm!*"[29]

"*Mon Dieu!*"[30]

"*Oy vey!*"

Someone grabbed Pinny's healing arm roughly. "Ouch!" Pinny's eyes filled with tears. Josh had been looking at a nearby display. When he heard the crashing noise, he came running over. Seeing the disaster area, the angry faces, and Pinny crying, he stepped forward boldly to help unravel the mess. "I guess we see the dangers of this resolution to global warming: humans falling onto the ships!" he joked.

Everyone laughed.

---

28   http://inhabitat.com/5-crazy-ways-to-save-the-planet-with-geoengineering/2.
29   Turkish.
30   French.

Actually, despite how it had initially appeared, nobody was upset at Pinny. They assumed that he fell. The only person who was upset was Pinny, and he was not upset at himself. Pinny made a quick decision. He would not tell Josh what really happened. Instead, he would do what he had originally planned. He would beat Eli at his own game: he would take revenge.

CHAPTER THIRTY-ONE

The plenary sessions filled with scientific talk were long and, for Eli, mostly boring. "Dad? Please? I'm hungry. I'll be back really soon!"

Richard Truxenberg waved his hand impatiently. He was focused on Dr. Arnold of England, who was presenting a fantastic report on the success of experimental glass domes constructed above the ocean-hugging cities of Bournemouth and Swansea. When Eli pestered him for the hundredth time, his father acted as he usually did when dealing with his attention-seeking son—impatient.

"Eli," he hissed in an angry whisper, "I told you before you came that you must behave! Look, I don't think it's safe for you to wander around alone. I'm a powerful person and someone here might see you and..."

"But, Dad, I just want to go for a couple of minutes and there's no reason to worry. I mean, there are tons of people around and there are security guards everywhere! I'm hungry and thirsty and bored!"

Eli's father knew his son's rambling list of arguments would continue. Eli had fully mastered the art of whining using logic.

Richard Truxenberg sighed deeply. Oh, how he wished that Eli would have gone to summer camp. But Eli didn't want to go. Originally, he was going to take a trip with his mother to the Catskill Mountains and spend the summer in their lakeside bungalow. However, her father, Eli's grandfather, had become seriously ill and Mrs. Truxenberg had to go to care for him. Since he lived in Crawford, Nebraska, a small town with little to offer in *Yiddishkeit*, there was no benefit for Eli to go with her. Richard had then tried to convince Eli to go to camp, but he was not interested. That left Eli in Richard's care.

"Fine. Go. But don't go far and come back within twenty minutes." Richard turned his attention back to the speaker.

Eli grabbed his father's jacket sleeve as he leaned over and gave him a quick peck on the cheek. "Thanks, Dad! See you soon! Don't worry, everything will be fine!" Eli cheerily sauntered out of the room.

❖

Dmitri licked his lips in nervous anticipation. Yuri stood at the entrance of the unused meeting room, serving as the lookout. The small room was empty, with a curtain covering the back wall, where there was the only other exit. Dmitri glanced at his watch for the third time in as many minutes. He would wait only five more minutes before he would assume that the clandestine rendezvous was compromised. The note given to him when he had first arrived at the Zappeion instructed him to come to this room at this time.

Dmitri distractedly rubbed his right wrist where a handcuff chafed his skin. A black pleather-covered briefcase was securely attached to the other end of the metal cuffs. It contained photos that would help Dmitri become a free man. Not just a free man, but also a rich man.

Dmitri stiffened when he heard footsteps. Yuri nodded once and a small, frail man, not the man who had delivered the note, entered the room and walked over to Dmitri, with Yuri following close behind. This man was also handcuffed to a briefcase. It was identical to the one Dmitri was holding. The yellow flower in his lapel also matched the one Dmitri sported.

"You have what I need?" the man asked.

Dmitri nodded. He fiddled with the combinations of the briefcase's double locks and snapped them open. Then he extracted a manila folder and opened its cover. A glossy photo of the completed nuclear propulsion cylinder stared back at them. "I have photos of the other parts to show you and the control room," he said in heavily accented English. "Now, what about your end of the deal?"

The frail man simply opened a cleverly concealed window on the side of his attache for a quick second. Dmitri caught a glimpse of the many green rectangles decorated with Benjamin Franklin's picture.

"That's $200 million?" Dmitri asked suspiciously.

"No. This is a down payment."

Yuri suddenly spoke. "That was not the agreement. Tell Mr. Woodrop that if he wishes for the plan to enter its final phase, we need to see all the cash!" At that moment, Dmitri realized that Yuri was sent along with him as more than a silent military escort.

The man's brows furrowed and his face darkened. "Quiet, you fool! Don't mention any names in this meeting! My client has serious questions about your ability to execute his plan. It's one thing to build what was ordered; it is quite another to make sure it works. My client has set up a Swiss bank account that will be accessible with the codes on the microchip that's in this briefcase. The chip has a time-delayed opening. Carry out what is required of you on time and the access will be yours. Otherwise..."

The arguing and threats issuing to and from the rumpled man and the rigid soldier increased in intensity. The ever-growing volume of their voices worried Dmitri.

Then, Yuri's hand began to inch toward his jacket pocket. Dmitri saw the slow, almost imperceptible movement. He knew that Yuri had a concealed weapon that had made it through the building's security, and he was fairly sure that this strange little man did too. Dmitri began to sidle toward the curtain covering the back exit. He was hoping to get out of the room safely in case any shooting began.

A loud sneeze made him freeze. It came from behind the curtain.

⬥

Eli had left his father with the hope of finding some excitement. At first he had headed back to the room with the displays and tried to have fun. But fooling around by yourself is plain boring. He began roaming the halls of the Zappeion. Eli was even desperate enough to want to look for Pinny and hang out with him!

Just when he thought he would die of boredom, Eli came upon a concealed door, like for waiters or something, and he pushed it open slowly. There was a beautifully embroidered curtain hanging in front of this entrance, which blocked Eli's view. But before making a noisy entrance and possibly stumbling upon a crowd of undesirables, Eli paused to listen. What he overheard shocked him. It was a plot to do something terrible, and that famous American Woodrop was involved! Eli figured he could become a hero! He had information about some sort of plot! He just needed to get out of the room and go to the police.

That's when Eli's nose began to itch. With the force of a runaway locomotive, Eli sneezed.

❖

Yuri stopped talking mid-sentence and a gun appeared in his hand. Frail Man's hand slid to the back of his waistband at lightning speed and pulled out his weapon. Both turned in the direction of the explosive sound. To their surprise, their guns were pointing at Dmitri!

To cover up his attempt to flee the room, Dmitri pointed to the curtain and indicated his intention to check out the source of the noise. He tiptoed over to it and then looked back at the others. The sight of the two of them standing with weapons pointed in his direction frightened Dmitri. He really hoped there would not be any shooting. If there was, the likelihood of his being hit by a stray bullet was nearly 100 percent.

Gently, Dmitri placed his hands on the curtain's pull chord and yanked it open. There was Eli, sitting on the the floor.

❖

Pinny was clapping, together with the audience, with all his might. Josh had just finished presenting his theory on climate change to the conference delegates. He had hypothesized that the climate issues were a result of solar activity.[31] Citing research of his own and of other renowned scientists like Dr. Feng Xueshang, of the Chinese Solar Institute, Josh displayed graphs and charts depicting temperatures on Earth as they corresponded to solar flares over the course of

---

31   http://www.breitbart.com/london/2014/07/29.

two hundred years. One year of unusually powerful solar flares was matched by a gradual increase in global temperatures for the next three or more consecutive years. Josh's work found support from many people in the room. Hence, all the clapping.

Slowly, the applause died down and people began to leave the room. There was a long break before the next presenter, and the masses went to find something to eat. Pinny stood up and tried to push his way through the crowd toward Josh. It seemed that people had lots to say to him.

"Pinny?"

Pinny looked up. Mr. Truxenberg stood before him. He looked worried. Pinny did not even know that Eli's father knew his name! "Excuse me. I just need to get to Josh before I get lost!" Pinny answered a bit coldly while trying to push past him.

"Pinny, please, I need your help." The pleading tone in Mr. Truxenberg's voice halted Pinny's advance. "Have you seen Eli? He went out well over twenty minutes ago and has not returned, and now I can't find him!" Richard Truxenberg actually sounded very concerned!

"I haven't seen him, but if I do, I'll tell him that you're looking for him."

Mr. Truxenberg took a deep breath. "Oh, I guess that's fine. I'll stay around here for now, so he can find me when he returns."

"Bye, Mr. Truxenberg," Pinny said, rushing away toward Josh. As he reached his friend, Pinny gave Josh a high five. "That was totally awesome!" Pinny exclaimed. "It was so awesome that even I'm convinced that we need to get the earth some sunglasses!"

"Thanks! You saw all those people who gathered around me after I was done? Clearly they were impressed with my evidence."

"That's fantabulous! Now what?" In truth, Pinny was discovering that all the topics related to global warming went around in circles: There is a problem. Nobody knows exactly what's causing it, but everybody has unrealistic and impractical ways to solve it. Of course, Pinny would never say this to Josh.

Josh straightened his tie and jacket. "Actually, Pinny, the ambassador of Italy has asked to speak with the US delegation about something. So as soon as I find Mr. Truxenberg, we'll begin. You have your phone with you?"

Pinny nodded.

"Okay. So get a snack and we'll meet here in an hour. If I'm not here, or there's any trouble, call me."

Pinny headed to the snack area and grabbed a bag of chips and a bottle of Coke. Finishing the food, he looked at his watch. He still had thirty minutes left with which to explore.

Pinny wandered around a bit until he came to the perfect place to check out. It was the little corridor in the back of the Zappeion—dingy and poorly lit. The walls were concrete and the floor was stone. For some reason, the area was deserted. Pinny walked along the hallway, peering into the doorways. These doorways served as service entrances into some relatively small meeting halls. Their purpose was so that a catering company or the convention organizers could conveniently bring items into the rooms without disturbing whatever event was going on. Pinny found it fun to look at the meeting halls from the wrong end.

He entered one of the darkened rooms. A flickering light at the other end cast eerie shadows on the walls. While standing there and thinking spooky thoughts, Pinny jumped suddenly. He heard voices in the hall and they were coming closer. From his spot in the dark room, Pinny could make out three men walking past him. Two were holding a bundle partially covered by a large tablecloth. The bundle was writhing. He heard one man say, "We should just kill him now."

The other said, "Can't do it without authorization."

"That's the problem with you weak Americans. We Russians solve problems quickly and efficiently!"

"And that's why you still live in poverty!" the other shot back.

The conversation became difficult to hear as the trio moved farther away. Pinny had heard enough to make him revert to his pre-bar mitzvah impulsivity. Taking care not to be observed, he slipped out of his hiding spot and followed them.

The men walked out of the building's propped-open emergency exit. There was a black limousine parked nearby. A chauffeur, seemingly standing around with nothing to do, stepped forward and opened the back door for the guests. The bundle-bearers shifted their bundle and unceremoniously dumped it into the back seat. As they did so, the tablecloth slipped and a head appeared in the back window. Pinny's blood froze. He saw it was Eli Truxenberg. Eli's face was a sheet of terror. Eli's mouth was gagged, offering him no ability to scream.

From his spot at the corner of the doorway, Pinny's eyes made contact with Eli's. Pleading poured from Eli's wide eyes. They were begging for his help!

Time seemed to slow down. Pinny watched as one man leaned into the back seat and hit Eli on the head, making him disappear from view.

One of the men, the tall and rigid one, said something to the driver, who closed the car door. The men briefly stood huddled together, conversing.

Pinny started to inch forward. His heart was beating as fast as a race horse's hooves on a racetrack. Perhaps he could get to the car and help Eli out before the men returned.

Just then, Pinny's mental hard drive opened up and he did a quick search for "Eli Truxenberg." There were hundreds of images and videos! One video began playing automatically.

Eli was standing over Pinny. Eli burst out laughing and then, with a cold gleam in his eye and a cruel smile on his lips, he replied, "No! I don't forgive you..."

Then another.

Eli picked up one of the ketchup packets and squeezed it out on Pinny's head. "Looks like you got hit by the storm!"

And finally...

Eli was racing toward Pinny with the puck. Eli's left shoulder smashed into Pinny's right upper arm. The crunch of broken bone sounded like a gun shot. Pinny's agonizing screams sounded like those of a gun shot victim.

These memories flashed through Pinny's mind in nanoseconds, courtesy of the *yetzer ha-ra*.

I don't have to help him! He's getting what he deserves! Hashem arranged it so I don't have to fight him myself! Pinny was practically shouting these excuses to himself. He did not want to listen to the voice of reason, the *yetzer ha-tov* that was trying to be heard over the insistent cries of the *yetzer ha-ra*.

Pinny desperately wanted to listen to his *yetzer ha-ra*. He wanted the sweet taste of revenge to fill his mouth. He wanted Eli to suffer horribly for the year of anguish he had brought upon Pinny.

But his *yetzer ha-tov* would not rest. "You are a *Yid*!" it shouted. "You have the mitzvah to help another *Yid*! Don't take revenge! Come on! Do you think that you'll be happy and enjoy the taste of seeing Eli hurt? Will that really make you feel better? Will you be able to live the rest of your life with the knowledge that you didn't help another *Yid* in his time of need?"

CHAPTER THIRTY-TWO

An epic battle raged within Pinny: good versus evil, right versus wrong. In the end, it was imagining the disappointed look on Josh's face if Pinny chose to follow his *yetzer ha-ra* that prompted Pinny into action.

Pinny again peered around the door frame. He saw the men's backs as they walked away from the limo, apparently heading to their own cars. Pinny watched as the chauffeur climbed into the driver's seat. Their confidence in leaving Eli unaccompanied in the back seat confirmed Pinny's assumption that Eli was unconscious and unable to help himself.

The car engine started. It was now or never. Pinny did not consider using the cell phone in his pocket. He actually stopped thinking at all. He just acted. Crouching, he raced to the car, reached up for the handle, and gently popped the door open. Quickly, he scrambled into the back seat. Eli was sprawled out on the floor, with blood oozing out of his split lip.

In the front, the chauffeur had just slipped the car into gear when the "door ajar" signal began to flash and beep. After the opening and re-closing of his own door did nothing to calm the incessant beeping, the driver decided to check the back door.

Luckily for Pinny, the fellow did not think to slide open the tinted glass partition separating his seat from those in the back. The slamming of the driver's door a second time as he left the car to inspect the rear door awoke Pinny to the gravity of the situation. If he were discovered at this moment, then he too would be a captive.

There was no time to get out of the car. Davening to Hashem that there was access to the trunk through the back seat, Pinny pulled on the backseat cushion. It gave way, offering Pinny a place of refuge. Pinny dove into the trunk and replaced the cushion as best as he could.

Then he held his breath. The back door creaked open and was slammed shut. Hard.

Two minutes later, the car was moving. *Now what?* Pinny thought. *This whole thing doesn't make any sense. Why are they taking Eli? Is his father so rich that it's worth kidnapping him? Or is his father so important in the government that people can make him their puppet by kidnapping his son? Why are they doing this?*

As he stewed about the matter, he felt the car finally come to a stop. Minutes later, muffled sounds told Pinny that some men had removed Eli's prone figure from the car and carried him away.

Chapter Thirty-Two

Pinny waited. He heard nothing. Well, actually he heard the sound of waves. Pinny panicked! Maybe they were going to put Eli in a boat! *I've got to get out of here*, Pinny thought. Cautiously, he pushed the backseat cushion out of its place and crawled into the backseat. Peering out of the window, he saw that the car was in the driveway of a villa standing mere feet from the shore of the Aegean Sea.

Pinny carefully opened the limo door and his heart nearly stopped. A piercing wail filled the air! He had set off the car alarm, and the alarm was doing its job of alerting the owner to an intruder. Pinny hastily dropped to the ground, gently closed the car door, and scooted under some brush on the side of the driveway. He lay there panting, gulping air as quietly as possible. Nobody came out to check on the car. He heard a couple of squelches and the alarm went silent.

As if that wasn't enough excitement for the day, the skies promptly opened up with a deluge. In his hiding place, Pinny was swiftly soaked.

Pinny pledged that he would donate twenty dollars to Kupat Ha'ir in honor of the *nes* that he had not been discovered. He fully realized now that he needed to be very cautious. Taking cover among the foliage growing around the villa, Pinny snuck up to the building and began looking through windows. One window was open. Looking around carefully and seeing that the coast was clear, Pinny climbed through it.

He was careful to walk along the edges of the room to avoid leaving a trail of water that would be noticed. The noise of the howling wind helped cover the sounds of the creaky floorboards.

Pinny stopped for a minute and listened. He heard muffled, angry voices coming from behind closed doors to his right. Pinny moved closer to the doors and placed his ear right up against one of them so he could hear.

"I tell you this was a big mistake!" a man bellowed. "It might derail the whole mission!"

"But Mr. Woodrop, the boy probably heard too much. He likely heard your name about the propulsion system and the money!"

"My name? Why would my operatives mention my name? Are they amateurs?! Anyway, my goals are to help people, not hurt them!"

"Sir," another, gentler voice chimed in, "I wasn't there at the meet, so I don't have any idea what the boy might have or might not have heard, but, well, I have a compromise to suggest. Let's leave the boy locked in the attic while we all go to the conference to be there for the dramatic moment. Then, when this is all over, we'll release him somewhere in the city. He's dazed enough from the shock and the blow to his head that he won't be able to identify anybody."

"That's a better idea…" Woodrop said.

Pinny wanted to hear more, but the sound of footsteps got louder as whoever was inside came closer to the door. Pinny dove yet again for cover, this time behind some potted plants.

In the next few minutes, the men walked out of the room, past Pinny's hiding place. When all was quiet, Pinny began to search for the attic.

❖

"Josh? I know I haven't spent any time with you during this trip and I apologize," Mr. Truxenberg said after their meeting with the Italian ambassador, "but I need your help." Mr. Truxenberg's brow was deeply furrowed with worry. "My son has disappeared. I have talked to security and nobody has seen him!"

Josh too, looked upset. "The truth is, I don't know where Pinny is either. He was supposed to meet me here. I tried calling him and it goes straight to voice mail."

Thinking for a minute, Josh went over to one of the security people. He asked to speak to the head of security.

CHAPTER THIRTY-THREE

Sam Woodrop stood in the back of the room. This was the moment he had dreamed of for years. A reasonable, albeit aggressive, businessman, Sam was unreasonably passionate about the planet. His feelings for the earth ran deep. Not only did he care enough about the world to not hurt the planet, but he wanted the earth to be there—and in good shape—for his grandchildren. He was fed up with the years of international conferences on global warming. All people ever did was talk, talk, talk! Well, now, thanks to his money, there would be a real change. Finally, global warming would be halted and perhaps even reversed, and humanity would be saved!

Woodrop had done his research. There were many opinions as to the causes of climate change, and Woodrop felt that he had found the nugget of truth in the muddy river. There were three clearly documented changes to the earth during the last century or so. Ocean currents had changed and were now delivering an unusually large amount of heated water to both the North Pole and South Pole, which among other things, was melting the glaciers there. Also, wind patterns showed that now generally weaker winds were evaporating less water, leading to less rain and higher earth surface temperatures.[32] Lastly, Sam's investigations showed that marginal shifts in the angle of the earth's rotation on its axis had the ability to cause dramatic differences in the greenhouse effects on the world. The scientists he had paid to study these matters indicated that if the human race could harness these three things, man could regulate the escalating temperature of the planet. So Sam had funded the creation of a master control center he called "C-WOP" (Controlling Wind, Oceans, and Planet), which exercised sole command over a rocket thrust system able to change the earth's speed of rotation as well as the earth's tilt on its axis, thus regulating the oceans and the wind with the earth's own shift.

Working with a group of Russian rebels led by some formerly high-ranking and still powerful Russian army officers, Sam had removed any chance that he would be blamed if there were any mistakes resulting from the planned demonstration. If anyone was blamed, it would be, albeit mistakenly, the Russians. Very few knew that it was his money backing the project.

Secrecy and anonymity were especially important, since his plan involved breaking various international laws and treaties. It would

---

32   http://www.pnas.org/content/111/40/14360.abstract.

likely have taken many, many years to obtain the legal go-ahead to build his special system, and, in Sam's opinion, there simply was no more time to waste. So, he took the bull by the horns, so to speak.

Now Sam watched with pleasure as Igor Vladenovich climbed onto the stage and made his way to the podium. Igor was one of Sam's most highly paid employees. Igor used to be a member of the Russian propaganda team before he was forced to flee for his life. His oratory skill was legendary. Sam knew that if *anyone* could make the world realize the value of Sam's contribution to the human race, it was Igor Vladenovich.

Igor began his talk. Beautifully weaving the three main issues together, Igor demonstrated the faulty thinking of the other scientists in the room and the futility of addressing climate change with many of the suggested solutions displayed in the hall next door. He convincingly argued that all of Earth's climate changes hinged upon controlling the angle of its axis, the wind, and the ocean currents. After twenty minutes, he had reached the climax.

"Therefore, my friends, my comrades, the day has come to refrain from talk. The hour has arrived to cease our endless meetings and put aside our imaginative conjecture. It is time to act! Now is when we begin a new, better, and safer era. The present is when we recreate a stable and everlasting planet.

"A wise and rich man has enabled us to research, develop, and build a unique propulsion system. We have named it *Padarok*, The Gift, since it is a gift to the world in order to save humanity from the horrors of global warming. *Padarok* is a specially designed cylinder embedded in the solid part of the Earth's crust with the ability to extend many stories above ground. Inside it there are twelve complex nuclear engines that heat liquid hydrogen, converting it into a highly pressurized gas. This heated gas is expelled through the nozzle at the top of the cylinder. The nozzle can be positioned to face almost any direction. The incredible amount of thrust expelled by the super-heated fuel will slow the spin of the earth by providing a counterforce to its natural rotation."

Igor used a holographic projector to display a 3-D image of the cylinder with a nozzle on top. The entire contraption was firmly embedded in a globe that was rotating from west to east. The nozzle was bent at a 90° angle to the east.

"As you can see," Igor continued in his most articulate way, "the nozzle will expel the gas parallel to the earth's surface. Watch."

Suddenly, a pillar of holographic flames shot out of the nozzle, frightening many in the audience. The computer-generated display showed the spin of the globe begin to slow, and after a couple of seconds of this intense exhaust, the model Earth actually started spinning in the opposite direction! The projector's 3-D model fired a second time and the entire globe's axis shifted. On the model, one could see how the movements impacted the ocean currents so the observer could imagine the consequences of changing the planet's tilting.

"This, my friends," Igor said, "demonstrates what we hope to accomplish. For us to achieve our goal of having full control, we will need to build at least three more of these unique mechanisms, placed strategically around the globe. Today we will demonstrate the power of just one. We hope this will prove to be the key to saving our future.

"At this very moment, our thermonuclear propulsion unit has become operational and the technicians are getting it ready. At the touch of a few buttons, the earth will slow its rotation just a bit. This will cause slight changes in wind direction and the flow of ocean currents around the world. This demonstration will be but a sample of the possibilities of this most valuable invention.

"Now I call your attention to the screen." Igor pointed to one that had appeared on the wall behind him. On it was an image of the

Chapter Thirty-Three

mountain that housed the special tube. "We have a drone flying alongside the site of our dear *Padarok*. It will broadcast live streaming video of *Padarok* in action. Momentarily, you will be able to watch how we plan to fix the climate crisis."

Igor finished his sentence with a smile and nodded toward Dmitri. Unnoticed, Dmitri had been sitting near the podium with his computer and an attached joystick. Dmitri now pressed some keys and moved the stick.

※

What Dmitri typed in Athens, Greece, set off a clarion warning bell under a mountain three thousand miles away. *Aa-oo-ah! Aa-oo-ah!* The alarm was followed by a robotic voice proclaiming, "Weapon engaged. Firing sequence has begun. Clear the area. Danger! All must find safety in Bunker 5. Firing commencing in sixty seconds."

This alert announcement was originally made in the era when the mountain served as a host for nuclear missiles. Even though the words were not accurate for the latest project in the bowels of the earth, it was decided that it was good enough and did not need updating.

The warning message repeated, and the voice counted down toward the firing, each time reducing the time left to find safety by ten seconds.

The few people, mostly dressed in military uniform, who had remained by the mountain, scurried toward the safety of the specially designed bunker.

The final alert was even more urgent. *Aa-oo-ah! Aa-oo-ah! Aa-oo-ah!* "Weapon engaged. Firing sequence starting NOW! 5-4-3-2-1. Fire!"

What followed was a tremendous creaking and groaning as the massive, 300 feet in diameter collapsible cylinder grew to its full height of 450 feet, reaching 100 feet above the rim of the mountain. The tube appeared identical to the 3-D model shown to the collection of scientists.

Considering its bulk, the five minutes it took as the mechanism of hydraulics and computer chips worked together to achieve this glorious height, was a paltry amount of time. As the towering cylinder locked into place, the earth shook. This quake alone brought tons of rock sliding down the mountains nearby.

Within the body of the huge, reinforced cylinder, multiple nuclear reactions began generating incredible levels of heat. In turn, the working fluid, in this case liquid hydrogen under pressure, passed through each of the tube's twelve complex nuclear engines, turned into a gas, and flowed toward the only exit available. The super-heated, pressurized gas was then choked through the throat of the nozzle on top, creating 44 million pounds of thrust.

The fascinated crowd watched with eyes glued to the screen. The sheer size of this man-made behemoth was a wonder to behold. They watched as the cylinder reached its full height and were awed as the super-heated hydrogen started to pour out from the nozzle. The bright hot gas billowing from the tube's nozzle created the image of a magnificent dragon exhaling.

They observed the continual increase of the ferocity of the super-heated gas. Then suddenly, without warning, there was a bright flash and the screen went black.

Loud chatter broke out among the assembled. Various comments could be heard.

"What happened?"

"*Ti symvaino?*"[33]

---

[33] Greek for "What happened?"

"*You ke'neng*[34] it is ah-h *jishu*[35] issue?"

In the confusion, Sam Woodrop left the room.

The *Padarok* promotion team had a protocol to follow if anything went awry. The planners knew that if things did not move forward as expected, it could only be because the equipment failed in a major way. While the planners had expected praise and encouragement when their idea succeeded in fixing the globe's climate, they knew that the world's wrath would fall upon them with any failure.

The rules stated that Igor was to stay where he was. There was little worry about him being in any danger. With his smooth tongue, he would be safe. Dmitri and Yuri were to immediately take all the equipment they could carry and make their way to the Russian Consulate for quick extraction.

Dmitri's cell phone rang as he felt Yuri's hand grasp his arm and lead him out of the front entrance. He was trying to figure out what could have happened. *What could it be? Did I make a mistake?* Dmitri's thought process was interrupted by the ground beneath him rolling. An earthquake knocked him off his feet.

The towering thermonuclear propulsion tube, creating thrust strong enough to move the world, had exploded! With the force of 100 megatons of TNT,[36] the detonation of *Padarok* sent a fireball soaring to the sky, visible from nearly 1,000 miles away and incinerating the drone that had been relaying the video of the momentous occasion. This blast was about 2,800 times more powerful than the combined energy of the bombs dropped on Hiroshima and Nagasaki. All towns located within seventy miles of ground zero[37] were obliterated. Window panes in cities as far as 900 miles away cracked

---

34   Chinese for "maybe."
35   Chinese for "technical."
36   A megaton of TNT is a quantity of energy released by an explosion.
37   Area closest to the explosion.

and crumbled. It was only the facts that the mountain was located in middle of an unpopulated part of the world and that the blast force went skyward rather than to the sides that kept the incredible amount of released radiation from killing millions of people.

The seismic wave created by the explosion measured 6.5 on the Richter scale. This quake, in turn, triggered other earthquakes for thousands of miles around. These quakes of varying intensity toppled buildings and roads, instantly killing thousands of people and making many more homeless. Even 3,000 miles away, in Athens, the seismic activity caused books to fall off their shelves, china vases to be knocked off their pedestals, and people to be thrown to the floor.

◆

Pinny was stealthily climbing a flight of stairs toward the attic when he felt the earth rock. The movement sent Pinny tumbling head over heels to the landing on the floor below.

With a new sense of urgency, Pinny raced back up the steps as fast as he was able, until he stood on the landing before the attic door. He tried the doorknob, but it was locked. He almost panicked when the earth trembled again. Looking around the landing, Pinny spotted a small, but sturdy-looking table near the wall. He paused to listen for any sounds down below, but he was pretty sure that everyone had left. He picked up the table and smashed it into the door with all his might. The old wooden door shattered with a loud crack, its middle panel destroyed, sending pieces of wood into the attic. Pinny frantically pushed through and wound up in a heap in the middle of the floor of the small, dark room.

Eli, sitting on the edge of a crate, did not move. His cheeks were tear-stained, and he was immobilized with fright. Pinny stood up and brushed himself off while his eyes took a minute to adjust to the dark. Once he located Eli, he walked over to him. When he heard sobs coming from this frightened bully, Pinny sat down on the crate and wrapped his arm around Eli's shoulder. "Eli? It's me, Pinny. I'm here to help you. Are you okay?" he asked.

Eli's sobs became more pronounced. As Pinny looked Eli's face over, he could see that the fright had left him. Eli's swollen, red face conveyed a different emotion: shame.

"Pinny," Eli's words began to come out all jumbled, and in between rasping sobs he said, "I am so sorry. I mean, thanks. I mean, I am so embarrassed! After all I did to you, and you still came to help me. You are a *tzaddik* and I…I'm…just…a *rasha*."

With these words, Eli let out a low moan and his body trembled with emotion. He put his hands on his temples and began rubbing. "My head…it hurts so much!"

Pinny just sat with one arm around Eli, letting him talk while he tried to figure out what their next step should be.

Pinny looked closely at Eli's face. His lip was oozing blood and there was a large lump on his forehead the size of a goose egg. Pinny was worried. Eli was in no condition, emotionally or physically, to descend three flights of stairs and run if they had to. Still, it was not safe to stay where they were. Even if there was no damage to the house from the earthquake, the captors might return at any moment and do something dreadful.

My cell phone! Pinny couldn't believe that he had forgotten that he could get help with the touch of a button! He reached into his back pocket. It was empty. A quick and frantic inspection of his other pockets revealed the sad truth. His cell phone was gone.

Pinny realized that now he had absolutely no choice. He felt the tremendous weight of the important task of saving his friend resting squarely on his shoulders. Never before had Pinny been challenged with such a great responsibility.

"Eli? We can't stay here. It's too dangerous. I need you to work with me." Pinny did not have a plan. He figured that they would just try to outrun the captors if they were discovered.

"Please stand up. I'm going to keep my arm around you and I want you to put yours around me." Eli stood unsteadily and the two wrapped themselves together. Slowly, they began the descent to the first floor.

They reached the landing on the second floor when they heard a roaring sound outside the house. Looking out of the small window, they saw a huge wall of sea water coming at them.

CHAPTER THIRTY-FOUR

Josh and Richard sat glued to the windows on opposite sides of the helicopter. Both were pretty impressed with the head of security. In an attempt to locate the missing boys, he had suggested that perhaps one of the boys had a cell phone. When Josh confirmed that Pinny had one, but it might not be on, the man had contacted the NIS, Greece's intelligence agency, and they had agreed to try locating the boys using their GPS satellites. But Josh was right. Pinny's phone was off and not emitting any signal.

Josh suggested they search from the air. "Perhaps they just wandered off and got lost. Two kids walking in the rain would be easily spotted from above."

At first, the NIS wanted the local police to handle it. But as the storm's intensity increased and the earth shook, manpower became stretched very thin, because the police were needed to respond to the tens of thousands of calls for help from the locals. The NIS decided that it made more sense to spare two intelligence officers. They would send a helicopter pilot and a copilot, rather than use many men to do a ground search for the missing boys. So Josh and Richard had been hustled to the police helipad and took on the job of lookouts. The helicopter flew in a grid pattern, carefully checking the streets of Athens.

The heavy rain decreased their visibility and increased their worries. Not spotting the boys during the last hour was giving rise to a feeling of panic. Only their faith in Hashem kept Josh and Richard from plunging into the depths of despair.

"Guys," the pilot said in accented English through his headset, "if we don't see something soon, we'll have to turn back. It's getting too difficult to fly."

At that very moment, Josh caught a glimpse of something out of the corner of his eye. He shouted into his mic, "Over there, on the roof of that villa. Someone is waving frantically!"

The pilot turned toward where he was pointing. Josh saw Pinny standing on the roof next to an open skylight. "That's Pinny!" he cried with excitement.

While the pilot hovered the chopper over the house, the copilot made his way to the back. He shouted to both men, "Okay, who's going down? I'm going to stay here and operate the winch." Josh volunteered.

"Come, let me connect you to this winch rope," the copilot continued. It was a little tricky in the wind-blown helicopter, but Josh, with

Chapter Thirty-Four   213

the help of Richard and the copilot, was able to fasten the special harness around himself and attach it properly to the rope system.

The copilot continued his directions in surprisingly clear English. "Here is a helmet. It has a built-in communicator. If you have any issues, just talk to us. We'll hear you and you'll hear us. Next, as you go down, keep your hands on this rope. I am going to attach a second winch rope to your harness, since I know there are supposed to be two boys. It may be feasible to get both of them out in one try, which is important, since the storm is making things difficult. I am also sending two harness belts with you so you can secure the boys to the second winch line and we can extract them from the building."

The rescue process began. As he was being lowered, Josh saw a wall of sea water racing toward the villa. He almost lost grip of the rope as memories flooded his mind.

From high above, suspended by a rope, with the noise of the helicopter in his ears, eight-year-old Josh watched as the second wave of water rushed toward his home. Suddenly, Josh let out a cry of anguish! The force of the wave swept it off of its foundation, and water completely covered it. Then the tremendous weight of the water caused his magnificent home to explode into a million pieces, as if it had been made of matchsticks!

Josh was yanked out of his thoughts by Richard's barking over his headset, "Josh! Why are you screaming? What's wrong?"

Josh shook his head to free himself from his nightmare. He had to regain his self-control. Then he gave Richard a thumbs-up. The winch continued to slowly lower Josh to the roof while he was buffeted by the strong wind. As he descended, he pulled the rope from the second winch along with him. Reaching the roof, he began to inch his way toward Pinny. He called loudly, "Pinny, are you okay? Where's Eli?"

"I'm fine," Pinny replied after he carefully inched his way toward Josh, "but Eli isn't in great shape. He's below in the attic. He didn't have the strength to pull himself up there. The bottom floors are already flooded and the house is wobbling!" Though he was right next to Josh, Pinny had to shout every word in order to be heard.

Josh helped Pinny into one of the special harnesses, attached it to the rope system, and showed him the correct way to grip the winch rope. "The copilot is going to pull you up. I'm going for Eli."

Without waiting for Pinny to reply, Josh signaled the copilot to turn on the winch. Then Josh pulled at his own rope to get enough slack for him to enter through the skylight.

Minutes later, Pinny was safely wrapped in a blanket and belted into a seat inside the helicopter. "Any sign of them?" he asked the two men.

"No," said Richard grimly. "They don't have much time left. That villa is not going to hold up much longer. Those waves are constant and the villa's brickwork is crumbling and washing away!"

"We're also running low on fuel. We can only remain here another few minutes," the pilot added.

Every few seconds, Mr. Truxenberg looked from his watch to Pinny. He knew how important Josh was to Pinny and he knew how much he loved his own son, even though he didn't show it enough. Almost unconsciously, he began saying *Tehillim*. "*Shir hama'alos...*"

As he finished his second *kapitel*, he saw some movement in the skylight below. Josh's voice crackled in his headset, "We're ready!"

The copilot immediately flicked the switch, and slowly the mechanical winch hummed and creaked as it lifted the pair toward the bowels of the helicopter.

Mr. Truxenberg shouted, "Here they come!"

They had some difficulty getting Eli into the helicopter. Although conscious, Eli was weak and a little disoriented from the blow to his head. It was only with Josh pushing and Richard and the copilot pulling that they managed to get Eli onto the floor of the chopper.

Once they were all settled, Pinny hugged Josh and would not let go. Opposite them, Richard, face shining with love and concern, sat next to an exhausted Eli, stroking his face lovingly.

CHAPTER THIRTY-FIVE

Two months later...

"Mesivta is so different, don't you think?" Pinny was sitting in the picnic area outside of the yeshivah building during the short break between *shiur* and *seder* with some of the other ninth graders. He was really thinking this, but the question somehow came out.

"It certainly is!" Yerachmiel Strauss answered. "The day is so long and even though we have less homework, I don't have much time for baseball."

"Yerachmiel, any school day longer than an hour is too long for you!" Pinny laughed. "I actually think high school is exciting."

Nesanel walked over to the bench. "Hey, Pinny, did I hear you right?" Nesanel teased. "Everyone is talking about the crazy adventure that you had during the summer. Now *that's* exciting!"

Azriel, who was lying in the grass, trying to soak up a few minutes of sun, raised his head abruptly and propped himself up on one elbow. "Yeah! I heard that you stole a limousine and were arrested by the secret police in Greece!"

Some of the boys started to laugh. "No! I'm serious! Isn't that what happened, Pinny?" Azriel insisted.

Pinny smiled. "Not exactly. I actually stole *into* a limo and got *rescued* by the police, I guess, kind of."

Pinny stood up to head into the school building. "Hey!" Azriel called after him, "you can't leave like that! Tell us the *gantze maiseh*!"[38]

"I won't be able to learn if you don't tell me! Please, have pity on my report card!" Yerachmiel begged Pinny.

"Maybe later. It's time for *seder* and I don't want to keep my *chavrusa* waiting."

As the group walked inside and entered the *beis midrash*, Nesanel could not help noticing that Pinny was different from how he was last year. Pinny was much more relaxed and even happy in school.

Nesanel wasn't the only one to notice the change. Rabbi Finegold had sat in on the ninth grade *shiur* on the second Monday of the *zeman*. He did this every year. He felt that he could share a lot of background information with Rabbi Pearl, the ninth grade *rebbi*, that might be valuable. However, Rabbi Finegold also wanted to make sure that the boys who entered Mesivta were basically the same ones who had left the eighth grade. Often, boys matured in their behavior

---

38   Yiddish for "the whole story."

and approach to learning during the critical transitional time right before high school. This change removed the need to share certain information, at least until an obvious issue arose.

Overall, Rabbi Finegold was impressed with the boys' learning and saw that they behaved much better. Their focus was great and their *middos* were right on target.

But the most impressive change that Rabbi Finegold saw was in Pinny. In the past, Pinny had been a relatively quiet boy in class, who paid attention but did not participate much in the discussions and was certainly not one to ask the *rebbi* many questions. That Pinny was gone. The Pinny who sat before Rabbi Finegold was confident and poised. He had his hand up a lot—to ask questions or to tell about the insights he had during the learning. He was also a happier kid.

Now, Rabbi Finegold stood outside the room, looking in through the glass panels in the doors at a marvelous sight. Pinny Gelbtuch and Eli Truxenberg were learning together. And they had smiles on their faces! Rabbi Finegold shook his head. He had heard about the adventure the boys had in the summer, but he did not anticipate that as a result they would become fast friends.

Still marveling over what he saw, Rabbi Finegold entered the *beis midrash* and went to the *bimah*. The time for *seder* was almost up and he wanted to speak to the boys in his capacity as *menahel* of the Mesivta before they went out for their break. He waited until it got quiet.

"*Rabbosai*," he said, "during the month of Elul, each boy in Mesivta takes on a project to earn more merit for himself by helping others grow closer to the Ribbono shel Olam. It can be for three months or longer. Last year we had some boys who adopted a nursing home to visit every Sunday. Others took upon themselves to tutor boys in the younger grades who were struggling in their learning. They did this for free. A *chesed*. There were a lot of great ideas then, and I'm sure you will come up with good ideas now.

"Once you decide on a project, come to my office and complete a project form. I will review your idea. If the idea meets my approval, I will place your name on the Approved List that will be posted outside the office. Once you see your name on the list, you may begin your project. Please remember that you will be asked to submit a written report about two weeks before Chanukah, detailing exactly what you did for your project on a practical level and what, if any, positive results came from your efforts. So keep track of your progress. Everyone who submits this final report is eligible—no matter how simple or complicated his project is—for a *sefarim* raffle to be held over Chanukah. If you have questions, feel free to come to me and ask. Now, go enjoy lunch."

His speech complete, Rabbi Finegold made his way out of the *beis midrash*. The boys closed their Gemaras and began to file out in small groups, discussing what the *menahel* had said.

Pinny, Eli, and Nesanel walked out together and made their way to the cafeteria. With their plates loaded with spaghetti, they found a spot at a table with other ninth graders. Inevitably, the conversation focused on the *chesed* program.

"I wonder what I could do," Nesanel said, twirling some spaghetti around his fork. "I mean, this is the kind of thing I know that my sisters have done in their school, but me?"

"Ask them," Eli suggested.

"I guess, but…" Nesanel thought for a minute. "Well, I will if I get stuck."

Eli looked at Pinny. "Do you have any thoughts?"

Pinny shook his head from side to side. "You?"

Eli scratched his ear, thinking. "I might," he said.

CHAPTER THIRTY-SIX

Richard Truxenberg sat at the dining room table with a *sefer* before him. His wife was in the kitchen, cleaning up from dinner. His gaze stretched across the table to Eli, who was sitting and working on some homework. A smile formed on Richard's lips and a sigh issued forth from his mouth.

"Is everything okay, Dad?" Eli asked as he closed his math book.

"Yup. Everything is perfect. Just perfect. I was just thinking, maybe we should go out for some ice cream."

Since Athens, the relationship between Richard and his son had changed. Richard had been a father who had focused on work and money. He had not been selfish. He had just wanted his family to have the best of everything. He had wanted them to lack for nothing. So as a result, he had ended up not having time to spend with Eli. Instead, his money did. Richard had thought that this was a good enough display of love to his son.

After the drama of the trip and Eli's complete recovery, Eli and his parents had held an intense conversation. The main subject was about safety and common sense. "How could you…", "What were you thinking when…", and other questions like that issued forth from his parents. This reprimanding prompted Eli to express to his father, in somewhat angry tones, "It's not like you really care about me anyway! All you care about is your work!" Eli's mother was taken aback by the hostility. But with great effort, Richard overlooked the *chutzpah* of the remark and focused on the message.

An hour later, Richard began to see the world through his son's eyes. Eli had shown him, with his father's encouragement, how time and time again Richard had put displaying love and caring for his son on the back burner. Whether it was by not attending Eli's school programs because he had to travel or go to a meeting, or by simply not listening to Eli's complaint about an issue with a friend because of an important phone call, Richard had let his son down. Now he saw his son's need for attention and desire to feel valued. Richard realized that although his wife had offered Eli all the attention and love she could, Eli still craved a relationship with his father.

And so, regularly now, Richard made it a point to spend quality time with Eli. They took walks together. They learned with each other. Sometimes they just talked in the kitchen over some cookies. Richard and Eli had become very close. Hence, the ice cream trip.

Ten minutes later, they were seated in the ice cream parlor with two double hot fudge sundaes on the table. "Dad?" Eli said after a few gooey spoonfuls. "In yeshivah today, the *menahel* told us about a special *chesed* program they run beginning in the month of Elul." Eli proceeded to share the details with his father. "I have an idea about what I want to do, but I'm embarrassed to do it."

"Eli, you can tell me anything you want and not be embarrassed. You've seen that I've been working hard on myself and on our relationship. Being a good father to you means a lot to me. You can trust me." Richard put down his spoon and gave his son his undivided attention.

Eli began. "You see, Pinny is a *tzaddik*. Even more so than you can imagine." Eli revealed how things had been between the two of them for a long time: Eli, the bully, and Pinny, the victim. He related details of the things he had done to hurt Pinny…how he had made Pinny's life miserable.

The entire time, Eli's father managed to sit there looking calm and actively listening to Eli's narrative without interruption.

"So imagine how I felt the moment that door to the attic in Athens exploded open and Pinny came tumbling in onto the floor. After all I had done to hurt and embarrass him, Pinny, who should have been glad to see me suffer, risked his life to rescue me!

"That moment really affected me. I realized how awful I had been and I promised myself then and there that I would change. As my friends can testify, I have.

"So when the *menahel* announced this program, I thought that I would like to figure out a way to convey to others how wrong it is to be a bully. I thought that maybe I would ask Rabbi Finegold if I could tell my story to the various classes so that boys who are bullies would maybe stop their bad ways. What do you think?"

Finishing his soliloquy, a very ashamed boy hung his head and covered his eyes with one hand as he waited to hear his father's response.

Richard was not sure what he should say. He was horrified to hear how awful his son had been. He also felt guilty about how he had neglected Eli—with this likely encouraging, if not directly causing, Eli's bullying behavior. He was also extremely impressed with Pinny's strength of character and courage. But he was pretty sure that the experts would tell him to ignore all that for now and focus on the question Eli had asked: Is this a good idea for his project?

"Eli, I think it's a great idea!" Richard was beaming as Eli raised his head and looked at him nervously. "I would be glad to help if you need me."

CHAPTER THIRTY-SEVEN

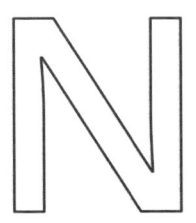

Not only was the Mesivta building on the same campus as the elementary school building, but they were connected by a long walkway. This enabled boys from both divisions to wander down the hallways of the other, causing little or no disruption.

For years, the lay leadership had been discussing the pros and cons of building a wall that would separate the two. Some felt that boys elected to attend other yeshivos instead of staying in the Mesivta because of this. Perhaps these boys felt that as long as they were connected to the elementary school, they weren't really going to yeshivah. Others focused on the money. As long as the two entities were not divided, Rabbi Finegold could physically serve as *menahel* of both. Dividing the buildings would require hiring another administrator. (Of course, nobody asked Rabbi Finegold what he thought.)

The educators knew that for ninth graders, having the buildings connected was a benefit. As the boys adjusted to the new schedule and less-structured environment, they took comfort in occasionally walking through the familiar hallways of the elementary school building. The "big" ninth graders would say hello to their "little" friends, shmooze with old teachers and *rebbeim*, and laugh to themselves about the rules they no longer had to follow.

Pinny found himself in the elementary school building the day after the announcement about the *chesed* program. He was using some of his morning break time to read some sentences on display outside the second-grade classroom, when he heard a boy crying behind him.

Pinny turned around to see if he could help. He saw that the boy was walking down the hall with his *rebbi*. Pinny recognized the boy as a sixth grader; he thought the kid's name was Aharon, but he wasn't sure. Pinny tried not to eavesdrop, but there was no other noise in the hall. He turned away and started to study the words in front of him, but the boy's pained words drew his attention.

"Rebbi, he's always picking on me! What choice did I have? Does Rebbi know what Yochi did to me during the game? Did anyone tell Rebbi how he embarrassed me in front of all of the sixth grade?"

"Aharon," the *rebbi* said in a stern voice, "I appreciate the problem and we will take steps toward solving it. But no matter what, the way you dealt with Yochi was wrong. Do you know that he's now in the nurse's office? His parents are going to have to take him to the doctor. Hitting him with your fists to stop him was not a good idea."

"But Rebbi," Aharon voice was shaking with sobs, "he's done something to me every day since the beginning of last year. I couldn't take it anymore! What else could I do?"

"I hear you." The *rebbi* sounded very concerned and caring. "But we need to discuss this with Rabbi Finegold."

As they passed by Pinny and continued to the *menahel*'s office, Pinny's mind raced. He recalled that not too long ago he thought that the solution to his problem was to get back at his tormentor. He understood now that, had he taken revenge, it was not likely that Eli Truxenberg would have become his good friend and *chavrusa*.

Suddenly, an idea for the *chesed* program began to form in Pinny's mind.

⋄

Later that day, during *bein ha-sedarim*, Pinny and Eli met outside of the *menahel*'s Mesivta office. They could hear the *menahel* talking to someone inside. Their *rebbi* had told them that Rabbi Finegold wanted them to stop by his office at the beginning of their lunch break.

"Why do you think Rabbi Finegold wants to speak to us together?" Eli whispered nervously to Pinny.

"I don't know, but let's get this over with." Pinny knocked on the door.

"Come in," Rabbi Finegold said as he opened the door, revealing two angry sixth grade boys sitting in front of his desk. "Aharon? Yochi? Could you step outside for a couple of moments, please?"

Rabbi Finegold did not give them a chance to answer. He escorted them through the doorway and pointed to two chairs in the hall. "Please, Yochi, you sit there. And Aharon? You sit here. I will call you back in as soon as I am done talking with these two *bachurim*."

Rabbi Finegold went back into his office and closed the door. As he sat down in his chair, he encouraged Pinny and Eli to sit in the

Chapter Thirty-Seven

now vacant spots. "Thank you very much for coming, especially since this is your free time. I must say that it is the clear *hashgachah pratis* of the story that motivated me to ask you to come today. You each submitted your *chesed* forms to me, and when I read them, I almost fell off my chair. Your projects were two sides of the same coin! I was impressed that each of you took such care in explaining why you chose your project, while trying to avoid any *lashon hara*.

"I was impressed that each of you wanted to use your experience to help others. Eli, you wanted to talk to classes about bullying and how wrong it is. Pinny, you wrote that you hoped to present to classes the best ways to 'handle' a bully. I spoke to the *rebbeim* and we want to work with you to come up with a good way for you to present your ideas together at the next Rosh Chodesh assembly.

"The *hashgachah* is that right now I have two boys in the hall who seem to be having an issue that is similar to what you boys went through. I thought I could convince you to begin your *chesed* in a more private way. I thought you could each work to help Aharon and Yochi resolve their issues. What do you think?"

Pinny and Eli shrugged their shoulders and looked at each other. "We could try." To their surprise, they had replied in unison.

The *menahel* smiled. "I will tell the boys that because of their fighting, they will need to spend the next few recesses in the *beis midrash* learning *Sefer Ahavas Chesed*. I will assign you as their *chavrusas,* as this is during your break time. This will give you the opportunity to guide them in a subtle and non-embarrassing way."

"Sounds good to me." Eli said as Pinny nodded his head.

"Great!" The *menahel* stepped out of his office and invited Yochi and Aharon back inside.

CHAPTER THIRTY-EIGHT

It was Rosh Chodesh. Pinny and Eli had presented their special program to the students of grades 5–8 when the Mesivta had Minchah, so they went over to the shul a few blocks away.

Both boys felt good about what had taken place at the assembly. They had met with Rabbi Finegold and a few *rebbeim* for a while during the days that led up to their presentation. The agreed-upon goal was to create a presentation that would encourage solutions rather than promote problems. The administration did not want anybody getting any ideas about how to become a bully.

Now, they walked into the shul's foyer and saw a crowd of adults listening to what the well-known lawyer, Mr. Silver, was saying. "Sam Woodrop is currently being tried by the ICC[39] in The Hague. I've learned that the authorities have apprehended a number of people who are willing to testify that it was Woodrop's money that funded that crazy exploding cylinder. They also have testimony that Woodrop hired the planners and knew he was in violation of many international laws relating to the transport and use of nuclear materials. To say the least, lots of people died and a lot of property was destroyed as a result of *Padarok*. This won't be over for a long time."

Pinny and Eli walked silently into the shul. The information that Mr. Silver was sharing was old news to them. Immediately after their dramatic rescue in Athens, the NIS had asked them lots of questions. When it became clear that Eli had information about the explosion, he was whisked away for more interrogation. It took the involvement of some high-ranking diplomats to ensure that Eli would not be called upon to testify against Mr. Woodrop unless there was a very compelling need. Richard was relieved when he had recently been informed that Eli's testimony wouldn't be necessary; there was enough evidence without him.

The boys each grabbed a *sefer* and learned while waiting for the davening to begin.

※

Josh was sitting at his desk in his new, small—but comfortable—office. The door bore a plaque with the letters GC³ embossed above the words: Joshua Green, Secretary. GC³ stood for the name of the newly created federal department, the Department of Global Climate Change Control, which had been commissioned by the

---

39   International Criminal Court.

president. As President Carl Almond had said, "It's high time that one of the greatest crises in the world has representation in the president's cabinet."

Across the hall, through his open door, Josh could see Mark Malone working out the day's weather predictions. They had not become close, but they were friendly. Josh made sure of that by going out of his way to have positive interactions with Mark. Josh did this out of his feelings of gratitude. He owed Mark something. After all, Mark was part of why Josh had his new job. Mark had given his recommendation that led to the trip to Greece.

Pinny and Eli had come to visit. Now that Josh lived in DC, the Gelbtuchs did not get to see much of him. Since the boys had a couple of days off from yeshivah for Chanukah, they decided to spend one of them in DC. The boys had taken the train from Penn Station in Baltimore and anticipated spending time at the Smithsonian with Josh. Currently, they were sitting across from him, reading copies of Josh's new book entitled *Global Warming, the Solar Impact*, as they waited for Josh to finish up some work.

The phone rang and Josh answered. "Hello? Office of GC^3."

"Hello! Is this Mr. Joshua Green? My name is Dr. Phil Prescott. My team and I have been studying the connection between the increase in super-storm frequency and intensity over the past two decades and global warming. I think that we have some valuable ideas to share with you. Could we meet?"

APPENDIX 1

THE TRUTH BE TOLD...

GLOBAL WARMING

The topic of global warming and climate change is often discussed at length and animatedly debated. Global warming is defined as "the increase in the earth's average surface temperature due to rising levels in greenhouse gases." Climate change is defined more generally as "a long-term change in the earth's climate patterns." Both are used by people to describe the warming of Earth over a period of time.

The basic explanation of the reason for the earth's warming that is most frequently given is that an excess of gas build-up in the earth's atmosphere, often called greenhouse gases, causes more of the radiation (heat) from the sun that bounces off of the surface of the planet to be trapped within the atmosphere. This heat is then sent back toward Earth instead of dissipating outside of the atmosphere. The more gas there is in the atmosphere, the more heat that is trapped.

The fastest increasing gas in the atmosphere is CO_2. Carbon dioxide naturally occurs there, but it is also produced by burning fossil fuels like oil and coal. The more factories and vehicles operating on fossil fuels, the more greenhouse gas emissions trap the heat of the sun and warm the planet. The hotter the planet, the more water evaporates from the oceans. This, in turn, is followed by more dramatic storms and increased melting of sea ice, which further leads to changing sea levels and even more severe weather.

Evidence that seems to prove that Earth is warming is countered by proof that it is not. While Artic ice seems to be shrinking, as visually documented in *National Geographic*,[40] Antarctica has had an increase in ice depth and volume; this finding is recorded by NASA.[41]

Even basic facts are unclear and subject to dispute. NASA has ten proofs that the planet is warming, and it is connected to humans.[42] Among the pieces of evidence is the following: "All three major global surface temperature reconstructions show that earth has warmed since 1880." Reading the source of the first study shows that the increase found was about .5°F—a small amount compared to what was anticipated. They write further, "The US has also witnessed increasing numbers of intense rainfall events." Yet Dr. Roy Spencer, a former NASA scientist, said, "Climate change has always occured... Severe weather has not increased."

The topic has certainly become a political issue and some suggest that a lot of the research presented by the government is compromised or tainted by politics. "No challenge...poses a greater threat to future generations than climate change," President Barak Obama declared in his State of the Union Address in 2015. Perhaps he is correct. But many experts vehemently protested this statement.

In *When the Ice Melts*, I followed the view of those who predict dire trouble due to climate change. Cities have been submerged and intense storms have become regular events. I exaggerated

---

40   http://environment.nationalgeographic.com/environment/global-warming/big-thaw.
41   https://www.nasa.gov/content/goddard/antarctic-sea-ice-reaches-new-record-maximum.
42   http://climate.nasa.gov/evidence.

facts to underscore the impact of the changing climate. However, I do not know who is correct. I only know that we say in *Tehillim*, in the second *Hallelukah*, that Hashem creates snow, frost, and ice; He issues His command and it melts them, He blows His wind and the waters flow.[43] The climate is in Hashem's hands.

---

43   *Tehillim* 147.

APPENDIX 2

BULLYING

Bullying is defined by many experts as unwanted aggressive behavior that is used to emotionally or physically hurt someone who is perceived to be weaker. It is not the common fighting and bickering found among children who are more or less equal. Bullying may include physical abuse, name calling, belittling, spreading false rumors, and intimidating another person. Besides the immediate pain felt from being bullied, the victims often suffer from long-term emotional scars, depression, and physical ailments. The victim feels powerless to stop the bully and is usually too embarrassed to seek help. Often the victim withdraws from school and friends as much as possible to limit the chance of being bullied and embarrassed. There are laws in every state regarding bullying, and a bully *could* be prosecuted, but often it is difficult to prove in court.

The most important first step for a person who is being bullied is to find an ally. An ally is an adult in whom the victim feels comfortable confiding, and the victim trusts that the ally will deal with the problem in a confidential way. This is not *lashon ha-ra*. It is being safe. The victim should describe the trouble in clear and specific terms, citing examples and providing names.

One of the worst approaches is to fight back physically. Typically, when the victim fights back, the bullying gets worse. In addition, when done in school, the victim likely gets suspended for this act of defense.

At the time of the bullying act, the victim should breathe deeply and assess the situation. What are his best options? One option requires building up the courage to state what he wants. For example, "Stop pushing me into the lockers and saying 'it was an accident' and then laughing. I know you can do whatever you want, but I want you to stop." Another is to walk toward a safe location, like a place with adults. Whichever will work should be employed.

Educators need to learn how to create an environment that is full of openness and trust to prevent bullying from developing. They also need to learn the correct way to help a victim through his experience as well as help the bully change his ways.

Parents play a vital role in supporting their kids if they are victims and helping children develop the caring personalities necessary to prevent them from adopting bullying behavior.

For parents and educators to learn these critical skills, there are many resources in print and on the Internet. A most valuable source is **http://www.thebullyproject.com**. It has tool kits for the student, parent, and teacher, as well as a fully developed program to sensitize and educate everyone about bullying, with the goal of making schools bully-free.

In this book, I concluded with the most important step to prevent bullying—talking about it.

ABOUT THE AUTHOR

Yechezkel Yudkowsky began creating stories in his teen years, enthralling his nieces and nephews with unique tales. Today, as a *rebbi* in Providence Hebrew Day School, Rabbi Yudkowsky weaves his storytelling talent with his teaching skill, instilling a love of school in his students while helping them retain the Torah they learn. He is currently working on his second audio CD in the *Sammy's Adventures* series, in which he tells an entertaining story about Sammy as he teaches about the laws of Shabbos preparation. Originally from Baltimore, Maryland, Rabbi Yudkowsky currently lives in Providence, Rhode Island with his wife and children.

To contact Rabbi Yudkowsky or to purchase *Sammy's Adventures: Sukkos Done Right*, please e-mail **torahdaycamp@gmail.com**.

ABOUT MOSAICA PRESS

Mosaica Press is an independent publisher of Jewish books. Our authors include some of the most profound, interesting, and entertaining thinkers and writers in the Jewish community today. There is a great demand for high-quality Jewish works dealing with issues of the day—and Mosaica Press is helping fill that need. Our books are available around the world. Please visit us at **www.mosaicapress.com** or contact us at **info@mosaicapress.com**. We will be glad to hear from you.

MOSAICA PRESS